Praise for Evolution

Evolution *is one of those books that will stay with me for a long time. I was sucked into the story from the very beginning and we need to have these books to support and educate our young people. Covering a sensitive topic about having a transsexual family member, this is a rare book and truly is quite strikingly accomplished.*
Emma Suffield
SLA School Librarian of the Year 2018
and Book Blogger

Loved it! Dan is a great protagonist. I think possibly a dad becoming a woman is hardest for a teenage boy to deal with. I love that reading this I felt like, yes, we are actually living in a world which is much more accepting of change, as Josh was unable to encourage the class to laugh with him at Dan. Reading Evolution *made me feel like the next generation of adults are going to make the world a better place!*

Joanne Spencer
WRD magazine

EVOLUTION

ZELDA CONWAY

First published in the UK in 2022 by ZunTold
www.zuntold.com

A catalogue record for this book is available
from the British Library

ISBN 978-1-9196276-7-0
1 2 3 4 5 6 7 8 9 10

Printed and bound in the UK by
Short Run Press Limited
25 Bittern Road
Sowton Industrial Estate
EXETER
Devon
EX2 7LW

For Dans everywhere

Chapter 1

Life sucks. School sucks. Teachers suck. Families suck, especially dads.

Dads suck most of all.

When Mum forgot to get me out of bed this morning, I knew it was going to be a bad day. She never forgets to wake me up. It always amazes me how someone as dippy as my mum can be so obsessed with being on time for everything, even stupid things like parents' evenings at school. Dad's more like me. If it was down to us . . . but there isn't any us. Not any more.

This morning, Mum crashed into my room just as I was in the middle of a dream. I was exploring the Amazon (not the massive online shop that sells everything from toilet rolls to tractor tyres) and I'd just discovered a new species of big cat. It was stripy like a tiger, but it had a mane like a lion. And its stripes were orange on black, not black on orange like real tigers. Very cool. It was looming over me, deciding whether to eat me, and I was trying my cat hypnotising technique on it, trying to persuade it not to. It works on Nelson, our ginger tom. All I have to do is wiggle my fingers in front of his face and make a noise like *woooooo* and he goes cross-eyed and falls asleep. I promise you. It's true. Anyway, it wasn't working in my dream and Dad was battling through the jungle, on his way to rescue me. I didn't think he'd reach me in time and besides, I didn't need rescuing. I'm nearly thirteen and I can look after myself, in real life and in dreams, too.

The tiger-lion was just about to pounce, and I was getting ready to wrestle with it, when something else dived on me. At least, that's how it seemed at first. I nearly had a fit. Then I came to a bit and realised that it wasn't a gorgon or a minotaur or anything like that. It was Mum, shaking me by the shoulders.

'Dan. You're late for school. Get dressed. Breakfast in the car in five minutes.'

I was quite bleary-eyed after the dream wrestling and the sudden wake-up call, but I thought that Mum's face was red and her eyes looked puffy. I hoped I was imagining it. Maybe I was still in my dream and this was a part of it. Maybe dream-Mum was mourning the tragic death of her dream-son after the tiger-lion had eaten him. She'd go on a crowd-funding website and get lots of money for a statue of me, and the fund would be massively over-subscribed so that she could put a statue of me in every town in the whole country.

No such luck.

They've been arguing a lot recently, Mum and

Dad. It always starts downstairs and then one of them throws a guilty look in my direction. I'll be staring at the telly and concentrating on it really hard, even if it's something rubbish for little kids, trying to block out the sound of their anger. Then one of them – usually Dad – says something like 'we should take this upstairs' and they stomp up and the bedroom door slams and within five minutes the yelling has started all over again.

I stumbled out of bed and pulled on my school uniform and trudged downstairs like a zombie. Mum was in the kitchen, slapping Marmite-smeared toast into a food bag like she wanted to suffocate it. Dad was – nowhere.

That was weird. Dad is always around in the morning. He works from home. He's a freelance software designer, which sounds really cool but mainly it seems to involve sitting in his 'office', which is actually the box room upstairs that's full of my old toys and some keep fit equipment that no one uses, in his pyjamas, looking at stuff on his laptop. He doesn't like sharing what he's looking at. I know that, because when I go in there to talk to him, he snaps the lid down really fast. Sometimes he does go to business meetings, though. Usually they mean that he has to stay away for the night.

'Where's Dad?' I asked.

Mum dragged one hand across one eye, smearing the black eyeliner she always puts on. Dad says she looks like Cleopatra when she wears it, or at least he used to. I haven't heard him say it for a while. Anyway, she smeared it down over her face, making her look like a vampire after a really bad day's sleep. I looked at her more carefully. Mum has this style that's part bag lady, part hippy. It actually suits her, so maybe I'm not describing it very well. But today, she didn't look like a cool mess. Just a mess. She had one of her long, flowery skirts on and a flowery top in completely different colours. She looked like the patchwork sofa in my friend Naomi's house.

'He's gone,' she said, with a sort of hiccup in her voice. 'Get your school bag. Here's your breakfast. We've got ten minutes to get you to school.'

'Gone? What do you mean, gone? Gone to the shops? Gone to the gym? What kind of gone?' I was getting a bad feeling about this. My insides were doing little somersaults. Where was Dad? Why wasn't he here? Why wasn't she answering me?

'There's no time now, Dan. We'll talk about it this evening.'

Now my insides were doing ginormous somersaults. I was scared to ask her what we'd be talking about that evening. I was willing to bet that it was nothing I wanted to hear. Maybe I'd done something to upset Dad. He'd asked me to clean his car last week and I 'forgot' but that wasn't too serious, was it? I'd get round to it, eventually.

Then she was pushing me out of the front door and into the car.

We drove to school in silence and it was like there

was this invisible brick wall between us. I wanted to ask her what was going on, but I was scared to. Mum kept giving me anxious looks and I could tell that she wanted to talk to me, but she didn't.

She wasn't concentrating on driving. She didn't notice the lollipop lady with the pink hair stepping out into the road, holding up her round sign. She had to brake suddenly so that she didn't run her over. The lollipop lady looked really angry, like Mum had done it on purpose and started mouthing rude things at her. I couldn't hear them, but I could tell by her gestures that she wasn't inviting her to tea.

Mum usually hates stuff like that. On a normal day she'd be winding down her window to apologise. Today, she revved up the engine and for a moment, I thought she actually *was* going to run her over. As soon as the lady with the lollipop had led a group of little kids across the road, and then collected a group on the other side who wanted to go the other way, making sure she took her time, Mum lifted her foot from the brake and we squealed up the road like a pair of bank robbers.

The worst thing was, when she dropped me outside school, she gave my hand a long squeeze. I hate stuff like that, and she knows it. That confirmed that something was really wrong. The last time she'd done it when it wasn't Christmas or something was when my grandad was going into hospital for a big operation and no one knew if he'd be coming out again. He did though. He's tough, my grandad.

'See you tonight. Don't worry,' she said.

Haha. That was like having a big scab on your knee that's just perfect for picking, and promising you won't touch it all day.

It just wasn't going to happen.

Chapter 2

School had already started. I could tell that straight away, because things were too quiet and there wasn't the usual pile of parents in cars, tooting at each other and muttering to themselves and building up their blood pressure.

Trying to ignore all the scary thoughts whizzing round my head, I went straight to reception to tell Mrs Chaudri that I was in, so she could add me to the register. She likes me. She always smiles when she sees me. Last month, I wished her Happy Diwali and she wrinkled her nose and pushed her glasses into place and said she didn't celebrate it, but she thanked me anyway. I could tell she was pleased.

'Daniel, *late?*' I like the way she calls me Daniel. No one else does. I needed her friendliness now. Maybe it would help to get rid of the butterflies in my insides and the feeling of disaster that I just couldn't shake off.

'Dad isn't well. Mum too.' What else could I say? Maybe it was true, at least the part about Dad being ill. After all, I didn't know what was wrong, only that something was. Maybe he had cancer? That was the scariest illness I knew about. Loads of people got cancer and it was always terrible. Some of them didn't make it. Was Dad in hospital?

Mrs Chaudri's eyes opened wide behind her glasses.

'Both? Nothing infectious, I hope? Should you be here, Daniel?'

'No, not infectious.' I was pretty sure cancer wasn't. 'I'd better get to class . . .'

I hurried away before she could ask me for more details.

My form teacher is Mr Hodges. He's big and round with a pointy nose and he always wears really bright ties. I think he looks like a giant hedgehog and that kind of goes with his name – Mr Hedgehodges – get it? I think that's pretty funny but no one else does, not even Naomi, who usually laughs at my jokes.

There are some differences between Mr Hodges and a hedgehog, though. The ties for one thing. And the other big difference is that hedgehogs are cute and friendly and Mr Hodges isn't. He's sarcastic.

My class is 8H and our classroom is on the far side of the main building. I ran through the corridors that sometimes smelt of furniture polish and sometimes of wet trainers (today it was trainers) and knocked on the door. There's a window in the door with some sort of wire squares in it, so I could see Mr Hodges sitting behind his desk, overflowing in his chair and talking. He likes talking.

His head turned and beckoned to me, but I had already pushed the door open.

'Daniel Yates! You've decided to join us! We're excited to see you, aren't we class?'

See what I mean about the sarcasm? A few of the kids sniggered – Josh Jacobs and Kyra McGee and that crowd. I've never got on with Josh. He used to try bullying me, but I've grown a lot recently and he's more careful around me now. He still doesn't like me, though. Most of the class just kept quiet. Naomi gave me a little smile and patted the chair next to her.

'Sorry, sir,' I said, not because I was but because I just wanted a quiet life. The last thing I needed today was hassle from Sarcasmo.

'Have you told Mrs Chaudri that you've arrived?'

'Yes, sir.'

'Marvellous. What intelligence! So, why are you late?'

'Parents ill, sir.' It was easier to stick to the lie I'd already told than admit that something was wrong at home. Maybe *really* wrong. That was my business, no one else's.

'Nothing fatal, we must hope.'

I hoped so, too.

'Sit down quickly.'

While he was droning on about rehearsals for the Christmas panto and changes to the lunch rotation and boring stuff that I never bothered listening to, Naomi ducked behind her bag, which she'd left on her desk.

'OK, Dan?'

I lifted my own bag in front of my face.

'Something's wrong. At home. My dad wasn't there this morning. Mum said he'd gone. Where can he have gone? He's always there in the morning.'

She opened her eyes wide.

'We'll talk at break,' she said.

Our first lesson was Biology. I really like it because it explains about how animals and plants work.

Today Mr Bennet was talking about the differences between men and women, which was a bit embarrassing, especially the video that he put on for us, but it kept my mind off my dad. We've done the subject before, of course, but it was still awkward to watch. Awkward and sort of exciting at the same time.

In the video, there was a real man and woman standing there, completely *naked*. Their faces had been pixelated, and no wonder. If I had to stand naked in front of a film crew, being filmed to show to millions of kids, I'd want more than my face pixelated.

'So, who can tell me the name for the man's sexual organs?' Mr Bennet asked, crossing his arms and leaning against the wall. He's cool. Maybe it's because he's quite young and he wears hair gel and stuff. Too cool for school, although of course he can't be, not if he wants to carry on in his job. But anyway, nothing embarrasses Mr Bennet.

'The proper *scientific* name,' he added, as Josh Jacobs shoved up his hand with a huge grin on his face. Josh Jacobs lowered his hand again.

Kyra McGee waved her hand.

'The *penis*,' she said, batting her eyelashes at him. Everyone knows she's got a thing about Mr Bennet and I think the eyelash batting was meant to look pretty, but it didn't work. It just made her look as if she was having a fit.

'Well done, Kyra. Do you need to splash water in your eyes? There seems to be something irritating them.' Naomi and me exchanged a grin at that. 'And the two round objects beneath it?' Mr B continued, after Kyra had gone the colour of a baboon's bum and shaken her head.

We got through the whole thing with a lot of giggles and nudges. Homework was to stick the sheet that Mr Bennet handed out into our Biology books, colour in the drawings of a man and woman with no clothes on and then label the sexual organs of both of them.

'Tastefully,' Mr Bennet said, with a glare at Josh Jacobs. 'Any jokers will find themselves in detention.'

At break, Naomi and me went to our usual quiet spot – a bench behind the swimming pool that never seems to get much sun, to talk.

'What's happened?' was her first question.

I looked at her worried brown eyes and crinkly hair and I wondered what to say.

'I don't know. But my dad isn't at home and my mum's eyes are all swollen like she's been crying and she's going to talk to me tonight . . . They've been arguing for months . . .'

Naomi bit her bottom lip.

'You've mentioned the arguing before. What are they arguing about? Have you found out?'

'No. They kind of hiss at each other and then when they get really agitated, they go upstairs so I can't hear. They don't seem to enjoy being together and they never do anything together, like couples do on TV . . .'

Naomi hunched one shoulder.

'My mum and dad used to be like that. I hated it. In some ways, their divorce was a relief. At least the arguing stopped.'

Divorce! I knew Naomi's parents had got divorced three years ago. She didn't talk much about it and I just took it for granted. It wasn't unusual. I reckon about half the kids in my class had divorced parents.

But – Mum and Dad – *divorced*? That was different. I thought about some of the things that me and Dad did together. When I was little, he used to take me to lots of zoos when Mum was busy or needed some peace. I think that's where my love of animals comes from. We went to Monkey World so often he used to joke that the day would come when they wouldn't let me out any more and I'd end up in a cage with the chimps. That didn't happen now because I was too old, but we still went to see movies together – *Star Wars* and *The Avengers* and other stuff that Mum wasn't keen on. He always bought me a huge bucket of popcorn and made me promise not to tell Mum. If the movie was rubbish and the cinema wasn't too full, we used to throw it at each other. What if Dad had gone for ever? What if I never saw him again? Who would I do stuff like that with?

What would it be like, having a mum and dad who hated each other and lived in different homes?

'Is it horrible – having divorced parents?'

She looked at me for a long time before she answered. I didn't mind the wait because I knew that whatever she said, it would be true.

'It's all right,' she said at last. 'You get used to it. Some kids really like it –they get two sets of presents at Christmas and birthdays, two summer holidays. Stuff like that.'

That didn't sound too bad, I thought.

'Do you see much of your dad?' I'd been to Naomi's house loads of times and I knew her mum but I hadn't seen her dad for years.

'Not that much now. It used to be more but recently he always seems to be doing something with his new family. You know he and his girlfriend have a new baby? Dad doesn't have much time for us.' 'Us' was Naomi and her brother, Michael. He was at sixth form college.

I got a tight, twisting feeling in my stomach when I thought about that. Naomi must feel second best – that she wasn't as important as her dad's new family. I didn't want my dad to get a new family. I needed him.

The bell went before we could say much else. The thought of going into lessons – of having to sit and do fractions and practise punctuation while my dad was out there getting a new family – was too much. I couldn't do it.

'Cover for me,' I said to Naomi. 'I need some time to think. If anyone asks you where I am, say my mum texted and asked me to come home and help. Tell them that they've got something serious . . .'

She opened her mouth to say something – probably to tell me not to do it – but I had to. So I walked off.

I had one piece of luck: Mrs Chaudri was busy in the back office when I went to reception to tell her I was going home, so I picked up a blue post-it note and a pencil and wrote: *My mum thinks it's leprosy. Gone to help them. Back soon. Daniel.* Then I drew a smiley face at the bottom so that she knew not to worry too much, and walked out of school.

Chapter 3

I'd never skipped school before. I couldn't see the point. It wasn't that bad. Now, as I walked through the school gates and turned left and crossed over the road towards Queen Elizabeth Park, I felt guilty, like there was a giant illuminated arrow containing the words *BUNKING OFF* hovering over my head.

I went through the big iron gates and past the beds with their sad pictures made from dying flowers. The park keepers or gardeners or whatever they were called must have spent ages doing them, but they were never that good and they never lasted long. They tried to make them fit with the time of year, so at Easter they made flower pictures of Easter eggs and in the summer holidays, of grinning suns. They were always a bit wonky or wrong in some way. The summer suns had been egg-shaped, not round, and the Easter eggs had been round, not egg-shaped. It was only because the gardeners had managed to make it look like they had pink and blue ribbons tied round them that I realised what they were supposed to be.

Today there was a new picture of a big baby. The gardeners hadn't left enough room for the baby's legs and it looked some kind of mythical beast – with a human head and body and two skinny worms instead of legs. I spent a minute wondering what a mutant baby had to do with anything before I realised that it must be Jesus, because it was nearly Christmas. The yellow halo round his head was the giveaway. I would have got it sooner if the halo hadn't looked like a bobble hat.

The mutant flower baby didn't make me think of Christmas. It made me think of my dad, starting life again with a new family. The thought made my guts twist. I wanted to cry, but I hadn't cried since last year, when my guinea pig, Roderick, died. *Be strong. You're nearly a grown-up. Anyway, you don't even know that Dad wants a new family. Or a divorce. Your mind is running ahead of itself.* My grandad used that phrase a lot and it always made me think of aliens or sci fi heroes, sending their minds out of their bodies and taking over other people's. Now I could see what Grandad meant. I was imagining all sorts of things that hadn't happened and maybe never would.

Without thinking about where I was going, I'd reached the swings. I must have been on autopilot. When I was little, Dad used to bring me here a lot. There was a man here now, swinging a baby in one of those swings with a bar that you bring down over the kid's legs so it can't fall out and crack its head open. The baby was wrapped up in a furry coat and it looked like an Ewok. Every time the baby swung forward, the man called out *'weeeeee'* in a really excited voice and the baby gurgled. They were loving it. It seemed that everywhere I went, there were hints that my dad was going to start again without me. That he'd be having a new family who would take my place. It was like the whole world was trying to tell me something.

'No!' I must have shouted the word very loud because the man with the swinging baby looked up at me. He bundled his baby back into its pushchair and walked away. I must have looked weird.

Coming to the park was starting to seem like a really bad idea, so I decided to go into town instead. If I stayed here much longer, I'd be seeing mutant babies in the clouds and puddles on the ends of dog leads.

Town was doing its best to look Christmassy, although it was only November. The crappy strings of fairy lights that they'd been using for about a hundred years had been strung up across the main roads. Most of them were twinkling but some of them had died, and that ruined the rest of them. Some men with a council lorry were pulling a big Christmas tree off the back of it, to put it up in the market square. It wouldn't be long before there were brass bands and school orchestras playing there at the weekends, trying to make people feel happy so that they spent more money. I just hoped that the tree would last until Christmas.

I went into WH Smith, rubbing my mouth and moaning a bit. I was trying to look like I'd just come out of the dentist's, in case I saw someone I knew and they wondered why I wasn't in school. Almost immediately, I saw our neighbour, Mrs Pollard, so I hid behind the felt tips while she looked at baking magazines. Thankfully she picked one quickly, paid for it and left.

Then the coast was clear for me to look for a new Manga. I found one and decided to buy it, although it would mean that I didn't have much money left to buy some food. I was starting to wish I'd stayed at school long enough to have lunch before I'd bunked off. I had just enough cash left for one of those cheap bars in clear plastic wrapping that look like birdseed in earwax, as well as the comic. Then I pulled my jacket closer around me and went to sit on a bench overlooking the square so that I could read my comic and watch the Christmas tree going up.

Before I dived into the comic, I did a search on my phone about DIVORCE. I was quite surprised at what I found out. Divorce seemed pretty popular and some people did it loads of times, almost like a hobby. Sometimes they made lots of money out of it, because everything they owned got split in half. I was confused for a second: how did you split a fridge in half? But it didn't take me long to work it out.

Maybe Mum would be one of the people who got rich from the divorce? If she did, I'd ask her for a new games console. And a mountain bike . . . But the people who got tons of cash from divorce didn't seem like real people – they were celebrities and princesses and things like that, and anyway, I'd rather hang on to my dad than get a new bike. I tried to count up all the kids I knew whose parents were divorced. It was a lot, and none of them looked as if they were that cut up about it. I felt a bit better and turned to my comic.

It was great. New characters and a brilliant double-page battle spread. For a long time, I lost myself in it and forgot about everything that was happening at home. I forgot my hunger too, although the birdseed bar hadn't done much to fill me up.

The comic was so good that I forgot to keep a look out, and to rub my mouth and groan from time to time, to keep up my cover story.

I was reaching the end of the comic, and was just sliding back into reality, when I became aware that someone had stopped, right in front of me. Someone big and round. Someone with a pointy nose and a Bugs Bunny tie.

Mr Hodges. He must have rushed into town as soon as school ended.

'Daniel. How's your parents' leprosy? Much better, I imagine, or you'd be at home, weeping over their death beds.'

Sarcasmo strikes again. If he was in a ninja comic, he'd have his head cut off on page one and he'd *still* be coming out with snarky comments.

I rubbed my mouth.

'I had to leave them for a bit. Dentist. Got a toothache.' I knew from spy movies that its best to stick to your story. It's when you start to add new bits to it that you trip yourself up.

'*Really?* Which dentist?' He had his hands on his hips, like my mum when she's giving me a lecture.

'That one.' I pointed over my shoulder to Hackett and Jones, the dentist we do actually go to, only not today.

'And you've just come out?'

He was falling for it. I nodded, gaining confidence.

'It took ages,' I said. 'Ouch,' I added, and rubbed my mouth again. I thought that would convince him.

But he gave his sarkiest smile.

'I'd better get on to the local paper and tell them about it. I can just see the headline: *Christmas Miracle – Local Boy Can Walk Through Locked Doors* . . . Hackett and Jones don't open on Wednesday afternoons. My girlfriend works there . . . You get on home now and check that your parents haven't lost any arms and legs. I'll be phoning them as soon as I get to school to enquire after their health . . .'

Chapter 4

I half expected Mum to be waiting on the doorstep, ready to start yelling as soon I opened the garden gate.

I was half right.

She wasn't on the doorstep, she was walking up and down in the living room, like an animal in a cage that's too small for it.

I could smell incense sticks, too. Another sign of trouble. Mum only burns them when she's really stressed and needs to calm down. She brings them home from the shop she works in. She says they smell of jasmine, which is a really strong-smelling flower, but all I can smell is a cross between a bonfire and toilet cleaner. It makes me sneeze.

'Mum . . .' I didn't know what to say.

She just looked at me and I tried to look back.

She was a mess. It wasn't just her eyes that were swollen, it was her whole face. She looked like a pumpkin. She must have been crying all day. I hated seeing her like that. It made me feel really useless – like I should have known how to help her.

'Have you had a phone call?' I asked. I thought I'd find out if she knew what I'd done before I started apologising for it. Maybe I wouldn't have to.

'Yes.' Her voice sounded thick, like she'd been eating porridge or mashed potato and didn't have anything to wash it down with.

'From school?'

'Yes.'

'Mr Hodges?'

'Yes.'

These one-word answers were doing my head in. 'I'm sorry, Mum,' I blurted out. 'About the leprosy thing. I've been really worried about what you said this morning and I just needed to get away for a bit to have a think . . .'

'Worried? All day you've been worrying over what I said. Gosh, what a useless mother I am! A useless mother and a useless wife. Just rubbish all round. No wonder . . .'

Her face creased up and she started crying again.

She obviously needed comforting, so I patted her on the shoulder. That would help.

'You're a great mum. The best! It's just – Dad – I've guessed about the divorce and him getting a new family and stuff . . .'

'*A new family?* Dan, there's no way on earth that your dad'll be starting a new family!'

'How can you be sure? If he's – got a girlfriend –' I

hated saying that to her – 'then she might want a baby. Especially if they get married . . .'

She gave a short laugh, which didn't sound amused at all.

'Believe me, your dad won't be running up the altar anytime soon.'

'But, how can you know, Mum? You're getting divorced, aren't you? I worked it out. All the arguing and stuff . . . You don't love each other any more, do you?'

I could feel tears prickling behind my eyes, but I wouldn't let them out. It would just make things worse for Mum. She must be feeling really horrible already, knowing that Dad had a girlfriend who he loved more than her.

She sat up then.

'Oh, Dan . . .' She pulled me down on to the sofa next to her and put one arm around me. My first thought was to pull away, but I stopped myself.

Then there was this long pause, like she didn't know what to say next.

'Dad's moved out, Dan. I don't know if it's permanent or not. It might be. It depends on a lot of things.'

'Out? Where?'

'He's renting a flat for now. A new one, in Abingdon.'

Abingdon wasn't far away. They had a good cinema there.

'Alone?'

She bit her lip and nodded.

'No girlfriend, then?'

'No, Dan, no girlfriend. Not as far as I know, anyway.'

Then another horrible idea jumped into my brain. If Dad didn't have a girlfriend, maybe Mum had a boyfriend? My guts churned at the thought. If she did, Mum might want to have another baby! She wasn't *that* old! I'd be stuck with a new dad, who I didn't want, *and* a baby brother or sister! The thought of seeing Mum with someone else, of her cuddling a baby that she could never give back, that was stuck in our lives for ever, made me feel sick.

I stared at her stomach. What if the baby was already in there?

'Before you ask, no, I haven't got a boyfriend, either.' She must be a mind reader!

Warm relief washed through my body, followed by confusion.

'But then, why?'

'Dan, there's no easy way of telling you this, but I have to.' She took a deep breath. 'Your dad wanted to tell you himself, but I thought that might be too much for you. He hasn't *found* another woman. He wants to become one.'

Chapter 5

'What do you mean? He can't be a woman. He's a man! He's my dad!'

I was on my feet, staring at her. I must have heard wrong.

Mum did something like a cross between a sigh and a shudder.

'It makes no more sense to me than it does to you. I've been trying to understand it since he told me a few months ago. He . . . wants to be a woman. Says he always has—'

'No! He's joking! Not Dad! If he's not joking, then he must be ill or something.'

Mum's mouth opened to reply, but I didn't want to hear any more. I ran. Upstairs, into my room. I slammed the door behind me and sat on my bed, but sitting down felt wrong. You sat down when you were relaxed. I stood up and walked to the window, looked out on to my road. Everyone was going about their normal business while my world shattered into little bits. I clenched my fists and breathed deeply. I needed to think. I was good at thinking, normally. I made myself sit again and thought about what Mum had told me.

Dad – *my* dad – wanted to become a – I couldn't think of the proper word for it. In town I sometimes saw a man dressed as a woman. It was so obvious. He got everything wrong. His shape was wrong for a start – rectangular instead of bumpy. And he needed some help with his make-up. It was too heavy. His lips looked like he'd put half a tube of paint on them. I saw people staring at him, nudging each other. He looked straight ahead, as if he hadn't seen them. I remember thinking that he must be really stupid if he didn't realise.

Sometimes I heard kids at school talking about him. Laughing at him. They called him the Lady Man. And now Mum was telling me that my dad was the same as him! It wasn't true. It couldn't be.

There was a knock on my door and Mum's head appeared round it.

'Maybe he's ill,' I started, before she had a chance to speak.

She gave a short laugh.

'That's one way of looking at it! But he says he's not. We've been talking about it for months, well, arguing really, and he says that he's always known. He tried to ignore it for a long time but he can't do that any more. The need to be himself is getting stronger and stronger . . . he says.'

Now I was feeling sick.

'I thought him leaving us and starting another family was bad! This is a zillion times worse. Well, he just can't, that's all.'

Mum put her hands up to her face and covered it. She looked like she was trying to hide her eyes from what was happening.

'He says he has to, that it's like the need to breathe. He's been trying to control it – going away to somewhere where he can dress as – himself,' she twisted her lips as she said that word ' – but it's not enough.'

So, all those times when he was supposed to be going to business meetings, he was really going to dress up as a woman! That was sick! And he'd been lying to us! And, hang on, what did she mean when she said that dressing up as a woman wasn't enough for him any more?

'So he wants to dress as a woman *here* as well as when he goes away? With us around? He can't. Never, ever, *ever*!'

Tears were streaming down Mum's face. I lifted a hand to my own cheeks and found that they were wet, too.

'Dan . . .' she didn't seem to know what to say next.

'What? . . . What? . . . Whatever it is, just say it!'

She kind of gasped and then said, 'Dressing as a woman's not enough for him any more. He wants to get the operations. To become a woman. For ever.'

'*No!*' I screamed it at her. I wanted to hit her. I took some really deep breaths, trying to calm down. Fish must feel like this, when they're caught on a hook and jerked out of the world that they know. You gulp and gulp for air, but it doesn't help.

'But what about us? What're we supposed to do?'

'He'd like to stay here. Still be part of the family. But I don't know if I can do that. And I don't know if you can, either. Neighbours would gossip. Maybe friends would drop us. And at school – kids are merciless. They'd pick on you! Laugh at you. He can't ask that of you.'

A horrible scene crept into my brain. Josh Jacobs, Kyra McGee and all their friends, pointing at me, mouths open really wide as they laughed at me. Their mouths were so big, I thought I'd fall in. And the noise of their laughter – HA! HA! HA! HA! HA! HA! It seemed to be drilling right into my brain. I shook the image away.

'Why can't you stop him?'

'I've tried, Dan. But it's no good.'

'It's not right. I hate him!'

This was too much for me. Too much knowledge that I didn't want and didn't understand. Mum was trying to put one arm around me again, but I threw it off like she really did have leprosy.

'I hate you, too! Get out of my room!' I yelled at her. She looked like I'd punched her in the face, but she stood up.

'You need time to think about this—' she began.

'Get out!' I was screaming like a baby and even as I was saying I hated her, I knew it wasn't true. But I just couldn't stop myself.

She sobbed like her soul was being torn out of her body, and left.

Then the guilt started. Of course I didn't hate Mum.

This wasn't her fault. It was all Dad's fault, and it was him I hated. I buried myself under my Avengers quilt and tried to blot out the world, but my brain was full of images of the Lady Man. Only now the Lady Man had Dad's face. That was the last thing I wanted to see, so I opened my eyes again and stared at the dark underside of my quilt. I stared so long, my eyes began to sting, but I didn't want to close them again in case I saw Lady Man Dad again.

I tried to think about what Mum had told me, but it was too hard. I just didn't get it. We'd talked about stuff like that in PSHE. Mr Hodges called it 'gender issues'. I thought it sounded weird but, well, live and let live. Another one of my grandad's sayings. If someone wasn't happy with their life and they knew how to fix it, that was fine with me, even if it sounded insane. Nobody sane would want to be a *girl*. But this was different. This wasn't just an idea we'd talked about at school. This was my dad. My family. My life.

I wondered what Grandad would think when he found out that his son wanted to become his daughter. He would be angry and hurt. Maybe it would give him another heart attack. Maybe he would die, and it would all be Dad's fault.

No matter how much I thought about it, it didn't get any better. It would change my life and I didn't want it changed. I wanted us to go on, just the three of us and Nelson, for ever. Or least until I grew up and left home. In the end, I put on headphones and played really loud music to try and block out the thoughts.

That helped a bit, especially if I did something else at the same time – so I threw darts at my dartboard and concentrated on trying to score a bullseye. I'd only done that once before, and that was when I was distracted by Dad suddenly opening my door, making me jump.

The combination of music and darts was blocking my thoughts pretty well, and I was still trying to hit the bullseye an hour later. There was a knock at the door just as I was taking aim. I jumped as I threw the dart. This time it missed, bouncing off the wire and dropping on to my collection of manga figures. They fell on to the carpet, looking like they'd just been killed in battle.

Mum was standing there again. I opened my mouth to apologise for saying I hated her, but I noticed that her lips were purply red, like a vampire's, and I stopped. I smelt wine on her. There was another glass of it in her hand. As she stepped into my bedroom, she wobbled a bit. She didn't drink much, usually, and the sight and smell of her now made me feel angry. She tried to hug me, but I stepped back. If she thought she could make me feel better with a hug, she could think again.

'We can't stop him, Dan. His mind's made up. He says he'll give us some time to get used to the idea before we meet his other self. His – her – name is Dawn. He's lined up an expert for us to talk to . . .'

That was enough. No, it was too much. I'd woken up that morning expecting my life to be the same as ever: to go to school, to learn some useless stuff, to have fun at breaks with Naomi, to come home and do my homework and go to bed and for the whole thing to repeat itself the next day.

But life would never be the same again. Yesterday was the last day of my normal life. Everything had changed for ever.

Over my desk there was a cork notice board. My lesson timetable was pinned up there as well as some more interesting stuff – postcards of animals and things I've cut out of magazines and newspapers about movies and games. There were some photos too: one of the three of us in Disneyland a few years ago, Nelson as a tiny orange blob, one of Mum and Dad when they first got together – they both looked really young and had terrible haircuts – and one of me and Dad on a sledge, that Mum had taken last winter.

When Mum managed to stop crying and had gone, I ripped that one down and stuck it on to my dartboard with a map pin. I spent the rest of the evening throwing darts at Dad. I skewered myself as often as I got him, but that didn't matter.

It took me ages to get to sleep that night. I was too busy trying to think up a plan for getting Dad to change his mind.

Chapter 6

Mum was still puffy faced the next morning. She looked really tired. I was sure that I looked like that, too. She asked me how I was feeling.

'How do you think I feel? I'm really sad. I'll be sad for ever if Dad does this. Tell him that, will you?'

'I will,' she whispered.

I thought about asking her if I could stay at home that day, but I decided that wasn't a good idea. At least at school there would be other things to think about.

We drove in silence.

As we pulled up, Mum turned and looked at me.

'Do you want me to ring Mrs Chaudri or the head or someone and tell them what's happening? They'll have to know at some point—'

'NO! Don't tell them. Not yet.'

What I meant was don't tell them ever. Telling them would make it real and I would start to be Dan with the freaky dad, instead of Dan who liked animals and anime and movies and stuff. It would change who I was.

She nodded.

'OK,' she said. 'But – they'll have to know sometime soon. It's important.'

I didn't reply. Instead I got out the car and grabbed my bag from the back seat and banged the door shut behind me. I didn't look back or wave or anything.

I met Naomi in the corridor on the way to registration. She looked like she always did – springing brown hair and the gap between her front teeth and the long, multi-coloured scarf that she'd been wearing since the weather got colder. I wondered if I looked the same as I did yesterday, when life was normal. I couldn't have, because she gave me one look and threaded her arm through mine.

'What?' she asked.

I couldn't tell her. Not because I thought she would tell anyone else. I knew I could trust her, but I didn't want her to pity me. I didn't want to lie to Naomi though. I decided to say something that was half true.

'I got into trouble for bunking off. I told Mrs Chaudri that Mum and Dad had leprosy,' I said.

She rolled her eyes.

'That was pretty stupid, Dan, even for you. No wonder you got told off! But what about your dad and the serious talk with your mum?'

I shrugged.

'Oh – he's lost his job. We've got to cut down on what we spend. They're gonna give me less pocket money until he's got another one.' That sounded pretty likely, I thought. Loads of people were losing their jobs at the moment. The TV news was full of them.

She wrinkled her nose, looking deep into my eyes, like she would see the truth there.

'OK. Well, that's a shame but he'll get another job, I'm sure. But why did you think he had left home?'

'He'd gone to a job fair in London, that's all. He stayed at a friend's house so he didn't have to pay for a hotel. Mum said he'd gone and I thought she meant for ever.'

'. . . OK, and you'd tell me if it was something more than that?'

'Yep.'

She gave me one of her long looks that meant she thought I was holding out on her, but by then we were in class and Mr Hedgehodges was giving me his snarkiest smile.

I remembered how nervous I'd been when I was walking home yesterday, after being caught bunking off. That seemed like nothing now. Now I *really* had things to worry about.

'How are your parents today? Still in possession of their limbs and digits?' he asked. He just couldn't resist it.

'Most of them,' I said, although I didn't know what digits were. I wasn't going to admit that to Sarcasmo.

Then he started yakking about the Christmas panto and how he expected us all to support it.

'As you probably know, I wrote it myself,' he said, looking so proud that you'd think he'd written

Shakespeare's plays instead of some crappy pantomime which wasn't even all that original, because he'd just chucked together some of the best characters from other pantos – Cinderella and Jack from Jack and the Beanstalk and the seven dwarfs but not Snow White. It was called *Where's Snow White?* Of course we knew – he'd been going on about it for weeks.

'Two of our form – Kyra and Josh – have starring roles!' he announced, like they'd won *The X-Factor* or something, and they both looked so pleased with themselves that I wanted to smash their faces in. They always got starring roles. Every year. If the play needed a princess, it would be Kyra. If it needed a knight in shining armour, it would be Josh. Kyra went to stage school and thought she was Ariana Grande or someone, and Josh was a soloist with the school choir, so it was no wonder. The panto would be more interesting if they *didn't* get starring roles, for a change.

'One of the cast has had to drop out,' the Hedgehog droned on, all serious, like he was announcing a national emergency. 'Tariq in 8B was going to play Prince Charming but he has an important family occasion and can't get out of it. Prince Charming is a fun role and there's no singing involved, so I hope some of you boys will have a go.'

'His costume is *really* gay – a pink satin jacket!' Josh Jacobs called out. And then he added in a stupid, girly voice, 'It's perfect for anyone who wants to dress up like the Lay-dee Man.' As he spoke, I thought he looked at me.

While the Hedgehog gave him a half-hearted telling

off, I felt my heart miss a beat. Did he know about Dad? Had someone told him?

My chance to ask him came on our way to PE. He was walking just ahead of me, pratting around to impress the girls.

I caught him outside the changing rooms.

'Why did you say that? About the Lady Man?' I asked, without wasting any time.

He raised his eyebrows.

'What? What did I say?'

'In registration. You said about dressing up like the Lady Man. Why?'

He threw a quick look at Kyra, who was standing next to him with this little smile on her face that made me want to chuck her fully clothed into the swimming pool.

'Oooh, Dan. Do *you* want to be a lady man? Should we start calling you Daniela?' He put on this funny walk that was supposed to look like how women moved. 'You'd be perfect to—'

That was as far as he got. I was so angry. I'd heard Grandad talk about the straw that broke the camel's back. I didn't know what it meant at first, but Mum explained that it was when things are getting worse and worse until you can't take any more and you give up. Or just lose it altogether.

The heavy knot that I'd had inside my guts since I'd found out about Dad twisted. I felt as if my whole body would burst into flames. My hands seemed to close into fists without me thinking about it and the next thing

I knew he was on the ground and I was on top of him, punching him.

'Dan!' I heard Naomi's voice and felt some hands on my shoulders, trying to pull me away and I turned round to hit out at them, too. Just in time I realised it was Naomi and stopped myself.

I took a really deep breath and she opened her mouth to say something else at the same time, but before she could I felt other hands – strong, like a man's – hauling me up.

It was Mr Harrison, the PE teacher. He's big and hairy and bad tempered, like a minotaur in a tracksuit.

'Daniel Yates. Get to the head's office. *NOW!*'

Chapter 7

Mrs Llewellyn, the head, was surprisingly nice to me.

'Is there something going on, Dan? Trouble with another pupil? Problems at home? This isn't like you.' She looked over her glasses at me and gave a little smile that somehow showed how serious she was.

I was sitting in her office in the big orange chair with the fake leather seat that the kids who'd got into trouble always had to sit in. I'd seen it before, when I got called in to see her so that she could congratulate me for getting a runner-up badge in a *Blue Peter* competition for designing a waterpark of the future, I never thought I'd end up sitting in it, though.

I shrugged and wriggled a bit. The fake orange leather squeaked. I was still calming down after my fight and I couldn't think of any words.

'And there was some trouble yesterday, I understand. You missed afternoon school and something about *leprosy?*'

Her eyes twinkled behind her glasses. Mrs Llewellyn has rosy cheeks and a soft Welsh accent that always sounds really peaceful. It reminds me of sheep and valleys and fluffy clouds. If there was someone at school I could tell about Dad, it was her.

But I just couldn't get the words out of my mouth. It would make them more real. But I didn't want to lie to her, either. I had this feeling that my life from now on was going to be full of lies about my dad, and telling the truth would be a treat. The longer it was before I had to start lying, the better it would be.

'There might be something wrong, but it's too soon to say. I'm a bit worried about it, though.'

She frowned.

'What kind of thing? Something serious? If so, I must know, Dan. You know that, don't you? I have a duty of care towards you. I would be failing in my job if I didn't try and help you.'

She looked at me all expectantly. She reminded me of Nelson, my cat, when he thinks I'm going to give him a *Dreamies* treat.

Just for a second, I imagined telling her and the look on her face when she discovered that my dad was a freak. The kindness on it would change to disgust or even worse, pity. I couldn't face it.

'I don't think it's serious but if it is, I promise I'll tell you.' Secretly I crossed my fingers because I was sure I would never tell her. It was too embarrassing. Much, much worse than having to stand naked in front of a load of school kids, like the people in the video we'd watched in Biology. People might forget that after a while, but I was sure that no one ever forgot when your dad decided to be a woman.

'I'll apologise to Josh if you like,' I said, knowing what the answer would be.

And I did. At afternoon registration.

'I'm really sorry, Josh,' I said, and in my head I added *that I didn't hit you harder.*

'That's OK,' he said, although the look on his face said something completely different.

Of course, the Hedgehog had something to say.

'You're not exactly covering yourself in glory this week, Dan.' His lips were a thin, straight line. The only thin thing about him. 'I think you've used up your quota of my patience for the rest of the term. No more, please, or I'll be calling your parents in.'

And wouldn't that give him a surprise? The lead weight inside my stomach got heavier at the thought of Dad turning up at school as a woman. But I just said I would try to stay out of trouble and then I went to sit by Naomi, who was giving me her under-the-microscope look again.

'There's something you're not telling me,' she said. 'Come to my house after school. You can stay for dinner and you can tell me what's really going on.'

'OK. I'll ring my mum.'

I liked Naomi's house. It was bright and messy and her mum was a good cook, much better than my mum whose idea of a nice meal was a load of grains and rabbit food with a lump of stinky fish dumped on the top.

I thought it was a great excuse for staying away from home. The longer I could do that, the better I'd like it.

Her mum was already home and we could smell something delicious cooking as soon as Naomi opened the front door.

Naomi's mum has a part-time job as a solicitor and she wears smart suits to work, but at home she wears leggings and baggy jumpers and that's what she was wearing now. The jumper was yellow and it suited her brown skin.

'Dan! Good to see you. Everything OK?'

I wondered if Naomi had told her that I'd been in trouble. No, she wouldn't split on me.

'All good, thanks, Mrs Honeyman.'

'We're going to do some homework in my room, before dinner, Mum. OK?'

'No problem. Take a drink up with you. It's a cold day.'

She fixed us two cups of hot chocolate and floated a marshmallow in each and we took them upstairs. My mouth was already watering. Naomi's daft dog, Spike, followed us.

As soon as the door was closed, Naomi started on me.

'Come on. Tell me the truth. I've been your best friend since nursery. I can tell when you're holding out on me.'

We were sitting on her bed, which had a cool duvet cover with a big picture of a leopard on it. Naomi was interested in animals, just like me. It was one of the reasons I liked her. We both want to be vets when we grow up and I was pretty sure that Naomi would be a really good one. Whatever she decided to do, she did well.

Why not? I thought. Why not tell her? She'll keep it to herself and maybe it will help. *A problem shared is a problem halved.* That was another of Grandad's sayings. He had one for every occasion.

I looked into her friendly eyes and took a deep breath. Suddenly, I really needed to tell someone I trusted.

'Please, don't laugh. You mustn't tell anyone. Not ever . . .'

Chapter 8

Naomi didn't laugh. And she didn't tell me to get out of her house because I was the son of a freak. She listened in silence, her eyes growing rounder and rounder. Something must have got in my own eyes and I had to wipe them a few times. After I'd done that, she took one of my hands and squeezed it.

Then we both sat and thought while our hot chocolate got cold and the marshmallows melted into pink swirls. Spike started lapping at Naomi's cup and she didn't seem to notice, even though chocolate's meant to be bad for dogs. In the end, she wrapped her arms round me and gave me a long hug. I didn't mind it, too much.

'That must be really tough,' she said in a quiet voice. 'I'm here for you, Dan. And I won't tell anyone.'

That made my eyes water again. Naomi had seen the Christmas tree in the market square and started talking about it, and that led on to the school Christmas party and the pantomime.

'Maybe I'll help out with it this year,' she said. 'Mum's always telling me to get more involved. There's a meeting about it after school tomorrow. Want to come?'

I said I'd think about it, but I couldn't see me getting involved, especially after Josh saying that there was a lady man in the cast.

After dinner, as I walked home, I felt the knot in my stomach growing tighter and tighter. Mum would be waiting for me and I was pretty sure she'd have a glass in her hand and her lips would be stained by the wine she'd already drunk. She seemed to live on it at the moment. I hadn't seen her eat anything for days, not even her usual rabbit food.

I wished I could stay at Naomi's but that didn't seem fair on Mum. It wasn't her fault this was happening. It was Dad's. Everything bad that had happened so far this week was because of him. I thought about bunking off school and beating up Josh and being sent to Mrs Llewellyn and about Mum living on red wine, and the anger in me that had died down while I was at Naomi's began building up again.

When I got home, I called out 'hi' to Mum and went straight to my room. I had homework to do.

I found my Biology book in my school bag and dumped it on my desk, knocking my manga figures on to the floor again. Then I sat down and stared at the figures of the naked man and woman with arrows pointing to their sex organs and the blank boxes I was supposed to fill in with the scientific names for them.

After a long time, I grabbed a pen and filled in the

names on the female figure. *Vagina, uterus, fallopian tubes.* Then I looked at the man and something seemed to burst in my brain. I scribbled all over his body below the waist until you couldn't see anything at all except angry black lines. They were so deep, they cut right through the paper.

I scribbled out all but one of the blank boxes, too, and in the one that was left I wrote the word *Freak*.

Then I shut the book, grabbed my darts and started trying to murder the dartboard.

It took me ages to get to sleep that night, even with Nelson purring like a little engine on my bed, and when I eventually managed it, I had a nightmare. I had gone to watch the school pantomime with Naomi, but as soon as we walked into the hall, people started laughing at me. I wondered why and I looked down and saw that I was wearing a dress. It was really over the top, with frilly sleeves and a sticking out skirt and a stupid little pink checked apron at my waist. I realised I was dressed like one of the Ugly Sisters in the pantomime Mum and Dad had taken me to last year. Everyone around me was laughing and pointing at me and I seemed to have trodden in tar or glue or something because I couldn't move my feet to run away.

I managed to drag myself out of the dream and lay in the dark, heart thumping, thinking about what I'd dreamt. What if I was like my dad? Maybe the nightmare was my mind trying to tell me that I was transsexual, too. Was it hereditary, like eye colour and sickle cell anaemia? We'd learnt about that in Biology. Was *I* going to be a lady man, too?

I tried to tell myself that I was being stupid, but the idea kept going round in my brain, like a toy train on a track.

I turned on my lamp and reached for my phone and played a game to take my mind off what I'd been thinking. I'd been playing it for at least an hour before I realised that it was pointless trying not to think of Dad. I might as well do some research.

I looked up the definition for *transsexual*. *A person who emotionally and psychologically feels that they belong to the opposite sex*. Seeing the explanation in print made it sound almost normal, but it wasn't – and the short sentence didn't cover the feelings of the families and friends who got hurt by someone who thought like that. There should be a special word for them, too. It wasn't fair. They were the victims in this. It didn't say anything about transsexuality being inherited, but then again it didn't say it wasn't either.

I kept thinking about what Mum had said – about Dad wanting to have operations to change his body so that it suited his brain. So I started to read about it, even though something was telling me not to go there. I gave up after about two minutes. My dad would be growing breasts. When I imagined Dad in a bra, with brand new breasts, I rushed to my rubbish bin and threw up. Then I closed my phone down, before I could see what else he would be doing.

After that I just lay there, hugging Nelson, and wishing that the last week was just another nightmare that I could wake up from.

Chapter 9

Naomi gave me a huge smile when we met the next morning. It was so big, it felt like another hug.

'OK?' she asked.

I just shrugged.

I was regretting what I'd done to my Biology homework but it was too late to do anything about it. Biology was the second lesson of the day, before break, so there was no chance of putting it right even if I wanted to.

I decided that my best chance was to hand in my book and make sure it was near the bottom of the pile. Mr Bennet wasn't always very good at marking homework. I think he was really busy at weekends playing rugby and drinking pints of beer and things like that. Maybe he would miss what I'd done. Maybe I'd be lucky.

At lunchtime, Naomi convinced me to come along to the meeting about the pantomime after school.

'It'll do you good to have something to think of other than your dad,' she said. 'You won't have to get involved if you don't want to. Just come and listen.'

I agreed because it would give me an excuse for being late home.

Our house felt empty without Dad, although there were reminders of him everywhere – photos and books and clothes in the ironing basket and his aftershave and stuff in the bathroom cabinet. I was surprised that he'd left the aftershave – it had been a present from Mum last Christmas and she said it cost a lot of money.

That made me think. How was Dad going to cope with his bristles? He shaved every morning. I'd seen a film once with a bearded lady in. She was in a circus and she looked odd to me. Was Dad going to look like that? If he did, I would die of shame. Maybe there was something he could do to stop his beard growing. A pill he could take? And what about his legs and armpits? I knew that Mum shaved those. Was Dad going to do that, too? Maybe he could use his aftershave on them, but I'd never seen Mum doing that. It was too much for me to think about, so I tried really, really hard to think about something else instead.

Apart from Dad not being there, I was finding it hard to be with Mum, as well. I wanted to say something to make her feel better, but I didn't know what. And she kept drinking more and more wine and I knew I should tell her to take it easy, but she obviously needed the wine at the moment and I couldn't blame her for that. If wine didn't taste like poison, I'd be drinking it too. If

I said anything it would make her feel worse than she felt already. So I ended up saying nothing and helping no one.

There were quite a few people in the hall after school for the meeting about the pantomime. The Hedgehog was in command, of course, prancing around and giving orders like he was Steven Spielberg or someone. Mr Bennet was there, too.

'I've volunteered to help with the stage management,' he said to the assembled kids, when the Hedgehog stopped speaking for a second to breathe. 'If you don't fancy acting, there are still lots of interesting jobs to be done behind the scenes.'

Of course, Kyra McGee's hand shot up at that, but Mr Bennet shook his head.

'You'll be on stage, Kyra. You can't be in two places at once.'

For a second, she looked like she was going to say that she didn't want to be on stage and that she'd rather help her beloved Mr Bennet, but the need to be the centre of the world was too strong for her and she closed her mouth again.

I wasn't going to volunteer for anything – I was only there to avoid going home and because Naomi had asked me to come – but when I thought about it, I decided that stage management could be quite fun. It would give me another reason to stay away from home. So I put up my hand.

'I'd like to help with setting up the stage and things like that,' I said. 'As long as I don't have to act.'

The Hedgehog looked a bit annoyed and I thought he was going to say that I couldn't help because of my behaviour that week, but Mr Bennet nodded.

'Great, Dan. Thanks.'

I was in.

Some others volunteered too; some to do make-up and others to help behind the stage or by making posters and selling tickets, things like that. Not Naomi, though, which surprised me after what she'd said last night about wanting to join in.

Then it was time for the auditions.

There was only one part up for grabs – the part that Tariq in 8B couldn't do now – Prince Charming. That didn't interest me, and I didn't fancy seeing a load of boys pratting around in a pink satin jacket, so I got up to leave. Naomi grabbed me by the arm.

'Don't go. Watch the auditions with me. It might be interesting.'

She looked into my eyes and smiled and I felt myself smiling back, even though I didn't want to.

I just nodded and we went to sit in the back row.

In the front row, Josh and Kyra were leaning back in their chairs like they owned the place. Now and then, they turned and looked at me and whispered to each other. I tried to ignore them.

There were only two kids who'd turned up to audition for the part – both boys. The first to try was a tiny Year 7 called Tom who was swamped by the pink jacket and was too shy to open his mouth. Mr H told him to try again next year. Then there was a boy from the year above us called Zak. He fitted the costume OK and even said some of the lines in a voice that we could hear, but he wasn't exactly charming. I think it was the way he stuck his finger up his nose halfway through the audition and kept it there.

'Anyone else?' The Hedgehog looked around the hall and just about everyone who wasn't already in the play looked at the floor. Just about everyone, but not *quite* everyone.

Naomi gave me a quick glance and then stuck her hand up.

'I'd like to try,' she said.

What? I swung round to look at her.

'What're you doing?' I hissed the words. 'Are you making fun of me?'

She glared at me.

'Don't be stupid,' she hissed back. 'It's got nothing to do with you.'

I didn't answer.

The Hedgehog didn't look any more impressed than I did.

'Sorry, Naomi, Prince Charming is a *boy*, in case you hadn't noticed.' He just couldn't hold back on the sarcasm. Having said that, I agreed with him for once.

'Who says so? Prince Charming is usually played by a girl in *professional* pantomimes.' Naomi's eyebrows lifted. 'And anyway, with equal opportunities and things like that, I think you have to let me audition. There are special police who check on stuff like that.'

That was news to me. I was too angry with my

so-called friend to stand up for her, but I didn't need to. It seemed that Sarcasmo believed in the Equal Opportunities Police, because he sighed and shrugged and told her to get on with it.

I had to get out of there. I couldn't sit and watch my best friend betray my trust by taking the mick out of my dad.

We stood up at the same time and as I turned to the door she hissed at me again.

'You need to grow up a bit. It's only a big deal if you make it one.'

I walked away without a word.

Chapter 10

On Saturday morning, Naomi texted me to say that she'd got the part. I didn't bother answering, partly because I was too angry and partly because Mum told me that she was taking me to meet the expert Dad had lined up. She was a counsellor, she said. I wasn't sure what that meant. I thought a counsellor was someone who knocked on your door on election days and asked you to vote for them if they promised to stop dogs pooing in the parks and stuff like that, but when I looked it up I found out that there was a difference between a *councillor* who was anti-dog poo and a *counsellor*, who listened to peoples' problems.

A good counsellor will never tell a client what to do. The role of the counsellor is to help the client reflect and find his own solutions, I read. That seemed pointless to me. Why tell someone your problems if they weren't going to help you? It was going to be a complete waste of time. At least, that was what I thought at first. Then I thought, *maybe she can tell me how to cure Dad.* That would make it worth going.

The counsellor lived a few miles away, outside Barstock, and I was pleased about that because I wouldn't see anyone who knew me. The last thing I needed was to be spotted by someone who knew that an expert in freaks lived there.

Mum insisted on coming in with me and although I moaned a bit, secretly I was glad because I'd never seen a counsellor before and I didn't know what I was supposed to do. Not that I wanted to go, but I decided that I'd go once, just to keep Mum happy. Not Dad. I didn't care if he was happy or not.

If you'd asked me what a counsellor would be like, from the images I had googled, I'd say old – at least forty. She would wear cuddly cardigans and have rosy cheeks like Mrs Llewellyn, and she would wrinkle her nose when she smiled, like Mrs Chaudri. I knew her name was Kim, but not her last name. The thought of calling a grown-up I didn't know by her first name made me uncomfortable, but I supposed it was just a counsellor thing.

As for her home, it would be as cosy as she was, with lots of photos of her family. In the toilet she would have one of those horrible crocheted toilet roll holders, like my gran used to make. They have a doll in the middle, grinning like a maniac. The doll's dress, which would be pink or maybe orange, goes over the toilet roll and her legs go through the tube so it looks like she's wearing a kind of fluorescent bad-taste wedding dress. They're pretty creepy. I'm surprised no one has used them as baddies in anime or manga. A host of grinning toilet roll holder dolls, chasing after you. That would *really* creep me out.

As soon as we pulled up outside the counsellor's house, I realised that things weren't going to be like I'd imagined. For a start, the house wasn't the pretty cottage I'd been imagining. It was new and square and made from plain white slabs of stone. The garden had gravel instead of grass and there was a big twisty metal thing in front of the house that looked like someone had dumped their rubbish there and run off, but I guessed that it was a statue. As we got out of the car, I looked at it from lots of angles, but I couldn't work out what it was, other than a mess.

A man opened the door. He must be a patient, I thought. He didn't look like a lady man, but then neither did Dad, at least he hadn't the last time I saw him. This man had grey hair, but he didn't look old, and he wore jeans and black shirt.

'Hi, you're Joanne and Daniel, right? I'm Kim.' He held out a hand to Mum and then to me. I shook it, feeling gobsmacked that Kim was a man. I felt quite grown-up, too. I'd never shaken hands with someone before.

Inside, his house was cool. He had a huge room with leather sofas and bright paintings on the walls of people with weird faces. Some of them had too many eyes and others had not enough. The coolest thing of all was a giant propeller, which must have come from a real plane, hanging from the high ceiling. I didn't go into the toilet, but I was willing to bet that there wasn't a knitted toilet roll holder in sight.

'Joanne, when we spoke on the phone you said you'd be OK with me speaking to Daniel alone. Is that still all right with you?'

Mum nodded and gave Kim a gooey smile.

'Whatever you think, Kim,' she said in a voice that matched the smile.

'Take a seat. Relax. There's reading matter here, if you'd like it.' He pointed to a table that looked like a giant cotton reel.

He led me to a door at the back of the house, into a smaller room. There were two sofas in it, not leather, very plain brown. He sat in one and nodded at the other.

'You OK with that one?'

I wondered if he wanted me to lie down. When I see psychiatrists on TV, they always get their patients to lie down. The sofas were the wrong shape for it, not long enough for a start and with no arms at the ends, but I decided I'd better do it anyway, so I leant back and tried to get comfortable. It was impossible because if my head was on the sofa, my legs were dangling over the other end and if my legs were on it, my head was stuck in space.

'You don't have to lie down. You don't look very comfortable.'

For a sec, I thought I'd say yes, I was comfortable, because I wanted to look cool in front of this cool man, but my neck was starting to ache so I sat up.

'I wasn't uncomfortable, but this will do for now,' I lied.

'So, do you want me to call you Dan?'

With most adults, you didn't get the choice. They decided what they'd call you. I shrugged.

'I don't mind.'

'OK. You look like a Daniel to me. Let's stick to that for the time being.'

The time being? If he thought I was coming back, he was in for a disappointment. I folded my arms.

'Tell me why you're here,' Kim said, leaning forward.

I shuffled on my sofa. I wasn't going to give him any help.

'You know why I'm here.' I leant back and folded my arms.

'Tell me.' Kim leant back and folded his arms, too.

I stared at him.

He stared back.

The staring seemed to go on for ever.

In the end I got fed up. I sighed.

'OK. We both know that I'm here because my dad wants to be a woman, and you're here to try and make me happy with that. But that's not what I'm here for. I want to know how to cure him.'

He wrote that down in a big red book that had been resting by the side of his sofa.

'That's not really accurate, Daniel. I'm here to help you *understand* why your dad's doing what he's doing and to give you the chance to ask questions from someone who knows about it. As to making you happy with it –

why would you be? If I was in your shoes, I wouldn't be. And I want you to try to stop thinking about it as something that can be cured. It isn't an illness.'

That was bad news. But I wasn't going to give up so easily.

'I'll never be happy with it. Not if I come here and talk to you about it for *years*. And how do you know there's not a cure? Loads of things can be cured these days. Even cancer!'

He smiled.

'Trust me on the cure thing, Daniel. It's not possible ,and if it was, what would give you the right, or anyone else the right, to stop him doing what he wants to do?'

I've got the right. He's my dad. I didn't say it out loud though. I could see that Kim wasn't going to be any help with curing Dad. So I said nothing. There was another long silence and then Kim said, 'People like your dad, what are they called?'

I thought of the Lady Man in town, with his wrong shape and bad make-up. I glowered at Kim.

'Lady Men. There's one in town. Everyone laughs at him and he doesn't even notice.'

He nodded.

'And the proper term for them? Do you know that?'

'Transsexuals,' I said, hating the feel of the word on my lips. It was the first time I'd said it out loud.

'Yep. Transsexuals . . . The Lady Man you've described? Why do you think he dresses like that? Walks around and opens himself up to ridicule?'

'Because he's a freak.' I could feel tears behind my

eyes. Before I knew it, they were flowing down my face. I wiped them away, furious with myself.

'That's one way of looking at it . . . If I told you that he knows what people think of him, that he deliberately looks the other way, what would you think of him?'

'I'd think he was a coward.' I curled my lip.

'I know him. Inside he's always felt that he was in the wrong body, like your dad. After years of unhappiness, he's decided to put nature's mistake right. To get the operations that will allow him to be a woman, to look like a woman, he has to live as one full-time, even though he looks a little . . . unconvincing at present. People laugh at him. Sometimes he gets beaten up. But he still does it, because he won't give up on what he believes in. Does that sound like a coward to you?'

I shrugged, hating him for a second.

He gave me another of his endless silences.

'No,' I said finally. 'That sounds brave. He's brave.'

He nodded.

'Yes. Brave . . .' He left a pause while I thought about my dad. 'Your dad tells me you're into animals. Want to be a vet, yes?'

I nodded this time.

'Think about evolution. When something in nature isn't right, or it could be bettered, animals evolve. Is there that much difference between an animal adapting to improve its chances and what your dad's doing?'

Chapter 11

Before I left, I dried my eyes so Mum couldn't see I'd been upset. When Kim asked me to come and see him again, I agreed, although I wasn't sure why. I also said I would write down anything I wanted to know about what Dad was doing and what was going to happen to him.

Kim walked Mum and me to the door and shook our hands again.

'Kim,' I said, looking at the twisted statue in his garden. 'What is that supposed to be?'

One side of his mouth smiled.

'What do you think it is?'

That was all I could get out of him. He said he'd tell me one day, or I could tell him when I'd worked it out. I got the impression that he was always like that – getting people to make up their own minds about things.

'How'd it go?' Mum asked, when we were in the car and on our way home.

'Not bad. I said I'd go again. I'm going to write down some questions to ask him.'

'Good idea. Maybe you can write down some for me, too.' I saw Mum's hands tighten on the steering wheel.

It was easy to forget that I wasn't the only one who was upset by all this. Mum was still drinking every evening and most days she woke up with a bad head and dark circles under her eyes. Until recently there had been a growing pile of wine bottles by the kitchen bin, giving off a sour stink. When I'd got home from school yesterday they'd disappeared and I wondered if she'd dumped them secretly, when the neighbours weren't around to see.

The thought of neighbours being scandalised by Mum's drinking made me laugh out loud. They were going to be a whole lot more scandalised pretty soon.

The rest of the weekend was pretty miserable. I ignored Naomi's texts and stayed in my room and played games and listened to music and wondered whether next week would be any better than the last one. I wondered if anything would ever be OK again, if I would ever feel like part of a family again.

Downstairs, Mum drank more wine and forgot to make meals and in the end I decided I would have to take charge. I'm not that good in the kitchen – I'd got into trouble in Food Tech when I tried to speed up making a casserole by sticking the chicken stock cubes straight into the kettle rather than pouring the boiling water into a jug. It made sense to me. But I was hungry and Mum needed a decent meal, so I decided to have a go.

She was asleep on the sofa when I went downstairs. Her eye liner had run. The TV was blaring and on the floor next to her was the usual wine glass with its little purple puddle drying in the bottom.

I went into the kitchen to see what I could find.

In the freezer there were pizzas and chicken pieces and ice cream and some peas and those greeny grey beans that are shaped like human foetuses, and a load of herbs that mum had frozen in little bags and a whole fish with its head and eyes still on.

I remembered that you had to defrost chicken first, otherwise you'd die of food poisoning, so I crossed that off the menu. As for the foetus-beans, they had outer coatings that tasted like chewy plastic and got stuck in your teeth, so they were a no-no. Cardboard tasted nicer.

I did get the fish out of the freezer and tried to cut its head off, but it was frozen solid and all the time the fish was staring at me with one flat, dead eye, like it couldn't believe how mean I was. For some reason that reminded me of something I'd read in a Horrible Histories book about someone who was being executed by having their head chopped off and the executioner made a hash of it and ended up sawing through their neck with his axe. That put me right off, and I wrapped the mangled fish up again and put it back in the freezer. Maybe I could blame it on Nelson.

So that left pizza, peas and herbs. And ice cream. Not exactly healthy, and the herbs were a waste of time. I decided to look in the fridge instead.

There were lots of eggs. Mum always buys them straight from the farmer and they had fluffy little feathers and poo stuck on them, which was a bit disgusting, but I picked out the cleanest ones. I decided to make Mum a nice omelette. She liked those.

I knew how to make omelettes, even though I hadn't had much practise. I beat the eggs together and heated a frying pan and melted some butter in the bottom. I think I overdid the butter, because the eggs kind of sat on top of it. They didn't want to cook. I turned the heat up a bit to see if that would help. While the mixture was getting hotter, I decided to get some peas out of the freezer to go with the omelette, and I got out the ice cream too and took off the lid to help it defrost a bit.

I cut open the pea packet and spilt a few. Well, most of them, actually. It was really cold and holding it hurt my fingers. I put some more in a metal bowl and stuck it in the microwave and turned it on and then remembered that you weren't supposed to put metal things in a microwave. I think it was the sparks flying off it that jogged my memory. So I took the peas out and swapped them into a china bowl and put them back in again. By that time there was a smell of burning coming from the frying pan.

I grabbed it and pulled it off the hob and lifted it up with a flat plastic thing like a fly swat to look underneath. It was burnt almost black, but the top was still runny. Then the peas started exploding like miniature bombs all over the inside if the microwave and I decided I'd better start again.

By the time Mum woke up I was ready. I felt quite proud as I carried the plate into the living room.

'I've made you a meal, Mum. Pizza and peas. I hope the peas are cooked OK. The pizza definitely is. I know you like them brown. There's ice cream after. There are a few peas in that, too, but they're healthy, right?'

She sat up and looked at the meal and started laughing and crying at the same time and she gave me a long hug and I let her.

We sat down together on the sofa and shared the meal and for the first time in a week, I felt like life was nearly normal.

Chapter 12

We'd finished our meal. Somehow the rubbish food had made us feel better. It was like when I was a little kid and I fell over and scraped my knee and Mum put an ice pack on it to stop it stinging. For a while, as we tried to carve through the rock-hard pizza and picked peas out of the ice cream, we forgot our problems.

There was an old movie on the TV about a man who gets shipwrecked on a mysterious island and finds that it's full of dinosaurs. The dinosaurs were as rubbish as my cooking and I'm sure that they were just normal-sized lizards with horns or frills glued to their heads.

We were just laughing, as the star tried to pretend that he was fighting with a dinosaur that was obviously just a projection on a screen behind him, when the doorbell rang.

We stopped in mid-giggle. My first thought was *Dad!* Judging by Mum's face she was thinking the same thing. But which Dad? The Dad I missed or the new Dad? The one I hadn't even seen yet? The freak?

I got up, but Mum put out a hand.

'I'll go.' I wondered if she was trying to protect me from the sight of Dad/Dawn. I was never going to get used to calling him that.

As she left the living room, she closed the door behind her.

I waited.

I heard voices. Mum's and another one. A man's, but I couldn't tell whether it was Dad or not.

I heard the door close and quiet conversation as two pairs of feet made their way towards the living room door.

The door opened.

'Dan. How are you?'

It was Grandad.

The way that Grandad walks is a bit weird. He leans forward and swings his arms a lot, like he's wading through mud. It's because his back got injured in a rugby match when he was younger.

As he waded towards me, I thought that he looked upset. He always dressed ultra-neatly, like he was still in the army, but now his tie was wonky and he hadn't polished his shoes – a serious crime in his eyes.

'I'm OK, thanks,' I lied. 'How are you?'

By now he'd reached me and he took one of my hands between both of his. I wondered why everyone suddenly wanted to hug me and hold my hands. I hoped it wouldn't last.

'Good lad, putting a brave face on it . . . I came as soon as I heard! That any son of mine . . .' He stopped talking and he went red, all over his bald head. He sat down and rested his head in his hands. 'A disgrace, that's what it is. A ruddy disgrace.'

Mum must have decided that I didn't need to hear that.

'Come into the kitchen, Ed,' she said. 'A nice cup of tea will make you feel better.'

But Grandad wasn't budging.

'Tea! I need something stronger than tea when I hear that my son's a ruddy—' He looked at me and bit back whatever he was going to say next. I was glad, but all the same I couldn't stop wondering what he'd been about to say. *A lady man?* Or something even worse?

'As for you, Jo, it's no wonder you're hitting the bottle,' Grandad nodded towards the empty wine glass on the floor. 'I've come to apologise for David. To both of you. And to say that whatever my son chooses to do – however he decides to live his life – I'm here for you. Don't you worry about that.'

'Thanks, Ed,' Mum said, although she didn't exactly look grateful, more annoyed. 'Let's get that tea—'

'I rang him,' Grandad continued, as if she hadn't spoken. 'In that new flat of his. I told him. I said, "if you do this, you're no son of mine! You'll lose your father as well as your wife and son. You've got no right to do this – you'll be ruining more lives than just yours." And you know me, Jo, I'm a man of my word. What I say, I do.'

'There's no need for that, Ed,' Mum said, after throwing a worried look at me. 'Don't say anything you'll regret. Who knows what will happen?' I think she was saying that for me as much as Grandad.

'I never thought I'd say this, but I'm glad Liz is dead and doesn't know what her son's up to. It would kill her all over again!' Grandad was back on his feet, wading across the rug, backwards and forwards. Suddenly he stopped and looked at me, then at Mum.

'This condition – it's not hereditary, is it?'

Mum gasped as she realised what Grandad was suggesting. Although I'd had the same idea, it freaked me out to hear the words actually spoken. I couldn't take this. I was on my feet and out of the room before Mum could say anything to make me feel better, or Grandad could do anything to make me feel even worse.

As I reached my room, I heard Mum's raised voice and then the front door opening and closing again. I sat on my bed and clasped my hands together. I hated this. Hated hearing Grandad saying horrible things about Dad, hated him suggesting that I might be the same. I had to find a cure for Dad. I just had to.

Five seconds later, Mum was knocking at my door.

'He's gone. I told him off. He says sorry, of course. He's going to come again next week, when he's calmed down a bit.'

'Is it?' I said, twisting my duvet cover round and round in my hands.

She didn't pretend that she didn't know what I meant.

'No! Of course not! Don't think about that for a second, Dan. I promise you—'

'Promise me because you *know* or because you're hoping?'

She looked surprised.

'Well, I haven't looked into it, but—'

'So you don't know. You're just hoping. This gets better and better.'

She sat on my bed and looked into my eyes.

'I'll look into it. I promise. But Dan, please don't worry about that. At the end of the day, we are what we choose to be.'

'I hope so,' I said. 'While you're looking into it, maybe you can look into what the cure is, too.'

'A cure? Dan, there is no cure. It's not an illness.'

I was sure Kim had told her that, just like he'd told me. But how could he be sure? I wouldn't give up.

I googled 'cure for transsexuality' and the results weren't good. Basically, all the people who sounded normal said there was no cure and got annoyed that other people thought there should be one. There were a few who thought it could be cured, but their treatments were things like 'placing your hope in Jesus, our lord and creator', or meditating and drinking stuff like dandelion juice and extract of spider bum. In other words, they sounded strange, delusional even. Not encouraging.

Reading all the bonkers stuff online made me feel sad, so I closed the links and played a game while I sorted out my thoughts. What I decided was this: OK, maybe there wasn't a cure for transgenderism (that's what the sane people had called it online), but that didn't mean I couldn't persuade Dad to change his mind.

From now on, that would be my focus.

* * *

When I walked into registration on Monday morning, Naomi was already sitting in her usual place. She'd kept the chair next to her free for me, like she always did.

I stood at the front of the class and looked at her and she looked back at me. She smiled, a bit nervously I thought. I ignored her.

The Hedgehog had walked in behind me. I didn't realise he was there until he tapped me on the shoulder and I turned around. He was wearing a stupid tie with green alien faces all over it. They were grinning at me.

'I'm sure there's a wide choice, Dan, but will you please decide who you want to bless with your company and sit down.'

I didn't say anything, just walked past Naomi and threw myself down next to Hannah Sullivan. She's a buddy of Josh Jameson's. Not one of his best friends, but she hangs around with him and Kyra. For a second, I thought she was going to tell me to take a walk, but I think she fancies me a bit – Naomi was always telling me that she did – and she just blushed and kept quiet.

Josh didn't though.

'Oh! Had a lovers' quarrel?' he said, in a soppy voice that made me want to start punching him again. 'What's the matter, Dan, has Naomi dropped you now she's got some cooler friends from the play?'

I'd opened my mouth to tell him where he could stick his snarky comments, but Naomi got there first.

'Something like that,' she said to Josh. 'Maybe I needed some more grown-up friends to hang round with.' She turned and looked at me. Her eyes were sparkling. I thought it was with tears.

I yawned and stretched, as if I hadn't got a care in the world.

'Whatever,' I said.

She turned back and her head went down on to her desk. For the rest of registration, I watched her and wished I was sitting next to her. But she was betraying me by dressing up as a boy. She must know it would upset me, but she was doing it anyway. She didn't care about my feelings and now my Grandad was waiting for me to turn into a lady man, just like my dad.

Was it possible for this week to be even worse than the last one?

It was certainly looking like it.

Chapter 13

I was meeting Kim again the following evening, and the BIG question was out of my mouth as soon as I sat down.

'Will I be like Dad? Will I inherit what he's got?'

Kim smiled and leant back on his leather sofa.

'Put it this way, Daniel, is your grandad transsexual? Was your grandma?'

I'd picked up a glass of water to hide my nerves and I was halfway through it. The thought of Grandad becoming a woman, with his army tattoos and bald head and tufty ear hair, made me gulp it down the wrong way. I coughed and spluttered and Kim had to bash me on the back. Grandad in a dress would make the Lady Man look like Wonder Woman.

'That's a no, then? Definitely?' I felt light-headed. I don't know if it was because of the choking or the relief of knowing that my fate wasn't sealed.

'It's a no. Absolutely not. If that thought has been worrying you, you can shelve it right now. And you should try to stop thinking about it as a disease. It's not.'

I didn't bother answering that, but for some reason I still felt a lot better. So good, that when Kim suggested that I should start thinking about going to 'meet' Dawn at her new flat, I didn't say no straight away.

'You've got two choices, Daniel,' Kim went on. 'Either you're going to have your dad in your life in some form or other or you're not. If you *are*, then I think you may as well get the first meeting out of the way. It'll be strange for both of you, *all* of you if your mum goes with you, but remember that nothing will ever change her love for you. Inside she'll always be your parent.'

So I said yes. Although most of me really didn't want to see Dad as Dawn, another part of me was curious. What would he, or she, look like? As bad as the Lady Man? Worse? I had to know.

As Kim walked me through his garden towards Mum's waiting car, I looked at the twisted metal statue in the garden and wondered if it was supposed to represent life. They were both complete messes and you couldn't work them out, no matter how hard you tried.

'He's agreed to go with you to meet Dawn,' Kim said to Mum, when she got out of the car to greet us. That annoyed me because it showed they'd been talking about me behind my back. But then, I should have known that. Mum went to see Kim on her own and of course they would talk about me as well as Dad.

'Thanks, Kim,' Mum said in the gooey voice she only used when talking to him. 'I'll make sure the meeting happens before he sees you again.'

I knew that Mum had already been to see Dad in his flat. She'd gone after work in the week and when she came home she'd hit the wine straight away. I asked her what it was like and I could see her trying to think of something positive to say.

'It could have been worse,' she said, swigging her wine.

Great. That helped a lot.

The meeting was set for Friday, after school. But the more I thought about it, the more I thought that I should see Dad by myself. There could be things I had to say that I didn't want Mum hearing.

Without Naomi, it was hard to decide if what I was thinking about doing was a good idea or a bad one. I was planning to go to Dad's flat by myself, before the Friday meeting. If he was expecting me, he'd be ready for me – looking his best. I didn't want to see him looking his best. I wanted to see what he looked like on a normal day – what other people saw when they passed him in the street. I wanted to see if he looked as obvious as the Lady Man.

The other thing was, I wanted a chance to reason with Dad. Just like he used to do with me when I was little. I remember one time when I was really small, I'd been watching a wildlife programme and I'd decided I wanted to be a tiger. I'd upset our neighbours by lying in wait for their toddler son, Alfie, and pouncing out on him. He'd screamed for about a month. I don't think that was why they'd moved away though. Dad had sat me down and asked me to think about how I'd feel if it was a real tiger, jumping out on *me*. That was how it felt for Alfie, he said. I would try the same tactic on him.

I decided I'd go to Dad's the following afternoon, after school. Mum had left the address of his flat on her note pad and I knew how to get there. I would tell Mum about it when I got home.

I got the bus from near the market square, where the Christmas tree was trying its hardest to bring some cheer into chilly, grey Cherrington and went upstairs. I was lucky – one of the front seats was empty, and I wiped away the condensation with my coat sleeve so I could see out.

The first thing I saw was Naomi, walking towards W H Smith with Lucy Barnes and Ashley Wicks. She was carrying a bag with some rolls of Christmas wrapping paper in it. They were laughing. I felt a twist of jealousy in my gut. Lucy and Ashley were in the pantomime, too. It looked like Naomi was getting on fine without me, making new friends and looking forward to a happy Christmas. Lucky her.

I sat back and lowered my eyes. I drew on my hands while the bus left Cherrington and went on its twisty journey through about a million villages towards Abingdon.

It was almost dark by the time I got off the bus. Dad's flat was in a new development, quite close to the movie complex. The development was called Fairweather Mews, which sounded pretty amazing. It wasn't. Fairweather Mews was just like any other block of new flats – white walls, white doors, white porches, white curtains in every window. Too much white. The designer had made the walls curvy at one end rather than flat, which I suppose was meant to make them look more interesting. Some of the windows were round, like portholes, for the same reason, I supposed. It seemed like a total waste of time.

I knew that Dad's flat was number 8, which was on the ground floor. Mum said that he had a private entrance, round the back.

As I walked round the side, past the tiny gravel patches that were meant to be gardens, I could feel my heart beating much faster than usual. My palms were sweating too, although it was pretty freezing outside.

All the time I was I thinking about turning around and getting out of there. Maybe this was a bad idea. I walked past a white door with a silvery number 6 on it. Then 7. Dad's was next.

And then I saw something that made me stop. Someone was hanging around outside Dad's flat. They bent down to look through the letterbox, then went to the window and pulled at it. It opened towards them, just a little bit. A burglar! Someone was burgling my dad's flat!

I crept closer. It was dark by now, but I saw a tall shape, in trousers and a short coat. The hair was long – a woman! I couldn't make out the colour of her hair.

If my heart had been beating hard before, now it was a drum solo. What should I do? No matter what Dad had done, I didn't want him getting burgled. We'd been burgled two years ago and I remembered how it felt – like our home wasn't ours any more. Mum had changed all the locks and left all the downstairs lights on for weeks afterwards.

I'm quite tall for my age – I take after Dad. But this burglar was taller than me. I didn't think that I could ambush her or anything like that.

I remembered what Dad had said to me after the burglary at home. I'd been having dreams about coming home and finding the burglars in the house. It had freaked me out.

'Just hide where they can't see you, make your voice low so you sound like a grown-up and say that you're from Neighbourhood Watch and the police will be here in two minutes,' he'd said.

I decided to try it now. I slipped into Dad's little porch to give me some cover. My legs felt like deflating balloons.

This was it. I could hear the window creaking as the burglar pulled it towards her.

'Excuse me, burglar-lady.' I was trying to make my voice sound gravelly, like a massive rugby player. The Neighbourhood Watch sounded to me like it would be a very polite organisation so I was trying to be ultra-civil, as well. 'I've rung the police. They inform me that they will be here in thirty seconds, so I think you'd better leave while you can.' There was no response from the burglar, so I added. 'They're bringing dogs. Lots of them.'

Chapter 14

'Ooh, I *love* dogs,' said a familiar voice. 'Maybe they'd like to come in and have a biscuit. You can have one, too, Dan. I've got Hobnobs – your favourites.'

My heart was doing really weird things today. Now it seemed to stop altogether and I wondered if I would die.

Then it started again and I took a step forward to have a closer look at the burglar. My brain was telling me to turn around and run before I saw something that I didn't want to see, but I ignored it. This was why I'd come here.

The woman had straight, shoulder length, brown hair with a fringe. She was wearing a red coat and black trousers and boots with little heels. She was carrying a red handbag. Her face was familiar and I was willing to bet that if I could see her eyes clearly, they would be blue, like mine.

It was Dad.

I opened my mouth, but no words came out.

Dad moved towards me, cautiously. He reminded me of Naomi's dog, Spike, when he's done something wrong. He's glad to see you but he doesn't know if he's going to get a hug or a telling off and he hedges his bets. That's another one of Grandad's sayings.

Dad lifted his arms, as if he was going to hug me.

That was a hug too far. I moved back. He dropped his arms.

'It's great to see you, Dan. I've really missed you.' His voice was still his voice, but a little quieter, like he had a sore throat or something.

Now I was here, seeing my dad, seeing how he wanted to spend the rest of his life, I couldn't think of a thing to say.

My eyes moved over him. He had make-up on, but not like the Lady Man. His was better, more like Mum's. He even had black eye liner on, like Mum always wears. I wondered what it felt like, smearing make-up on your face. I looked at his smooth chin and plucked eyebrows, peeking out from under his fringe.

'Does it hurt?' I asked. My voice sounded as quiet as his.

Dad frowned.

'Does what hurt?'

'Plucking your eyebrows, sorting out your chin hair, stuff like that.'

He gave a little laugh and one of his gloved hands went up to his chin.

'Bloody painful. But I'm told it gets less painful over time.'

Who was he talking to about such private things? Mum? Kim?

'Who told you that?'

'Friends. Supportive friends of both sexes, many of them just like me.'

That astonished me. How many more lady men and men ladies could there be? Maybe Kim hadn't been straight with me and becoming transsexual was catching, like measles.

'In *Cherrington?*'

Dad laughed again.

'A few, yes, and all around the country. There's an organisation in London that helps people like me. I met my friends through that.'

That sounded like a bad joke. I imagined them all, a building full of freaks, staggering to work in heels that they couldn't walk in, or in men's clothes that were too big for them. It sounded like a circus parade. I wondered if crowds gathered every day to have a laugh at them.

'Why?' I asked.

'Why what?'

'You know what. Why are you doing this? Ruining our family? Making yourself into a freak? Making Mum and me miserable?'

He made a big, shaky sigh.

'Can we talk about this inside? Where it's warm and private? I'm turning into an ice block, standing here.'

'Through the window?' I asked.

He smiled, and when he did he looked just like Dad again. I felt my heart cracking.

'I'll go through the window. You wait here for a sec and I'll open the door for you . . .'

He pulled the window further towards him and climbed through. A second later, the door opened.

'Forgot my key – it's in my other handbag. You know me, I'd forgot my head if it wasn't attached to my shoulders.'

At the mention of handbags, my heart cracked a little more. Once more, I thought about walking away, but Dad was smiling at me and holding the door wide open.

'It's a bit of a mess, I'm afraid. I was going to tidy up for you tomorrow . . .'

Dad's flat was kind of like our house. The walls were that colour that isn't quite white and there were two big pictures leaning against them, ready to be hung up. One was a photo of a lighthouse with a crashing sea and the other was a painting of a butterfly. There was a plain sofa in green, long enough to lie full length on, and another chair that didn't match it. There were rugs on the carpet and a big mirror in a fancy silver frame over the fire place. The fire in it was one of those grotty artificial ones, not a real one like at home. There were two or three little supermarket plants, still in their clear plastic wrappers, looking like they needed watering.

It wasn't a mess though. It was much tidier than Dad had been when he was still Dad. His office had always been full of stone-cold cups with coffee puddles in the bottom and screwed up balls of paper that he'd thrown at the bin and missed.

'Take a seat. I'll get those biscuits. Fancy a hot chocolate?'

I nodded and sat in the chair. That way, Dad wouldn't be able to sit too close to me. There was a little carved table next to it that looked Indian or something. It was the sort of thing Mum would like. On top of it there was a framed photo of the three of us: Mum, Dad and me. Actually, Nelson was in the photo too, a tiny kitten cuddling into Mum's arms, so that meant the whole family was there.

I stared at the photo for a long time. I don't know how long I was looking at it, but it must have been quite a few minutes. When I looked up, Dad was sitting opposite me, one leg crossed over the other like a woman sits, and two cups of cocoa were steaming on the coffee table. He'd brought in the Hobnobs, too.

I found it hard to look at him, so I took a Hobnob and examined that instead. There was a long silence and eventually I looked up to see Dad staring at me. I reckon he learned that trick – the long silence trick – from Kim.

There was so much I wanted to ask him, but I was scared. So instead I said something safe.

'Kim's nice.'

'Yes, he is. I'm glad you get on with him.'

Silence again.

'Mum likes him, too.'

'Good.'

Another pause. Dad was watching me. I stared at his boots. They were the kind of boots Mrs Llewellyn wore – black and plain with square heels, not very high.

'Are those easy to walk in?' I asked, when I couldn't bear the silence any more.

'You get used to them. I've been practising for a long time.'

That made me look up.

'So Mum said. You've been doing this all the time – all the time you were pretending to be my dad, pretending to be at business meetings, pretending to be a man . . .' I could feel tears brimming and I sniffed them back, angrily.

Dad held up one hand. Although his palm was towards me, I caught a glimpse of nails varnished red to match his coat and it felt as if they were tearing into my heart.

'Woah, Dan. I wasn't pretending. I *AM* your dad, and I *AM* married to your mum. I'd like to carry on being those things, if you'll let me. I just need to do this as well. When I don't do it, I feel like I'm in fancy dress – pretending to be David Yates. Imagine what that feels like – never being yourself, always keeping up a pretence. It was like being a spy, wondering every second when I was going to get caught and when the world would end.'

The words were tumbling out of him now, but I couldn't sit there and listen. All the anger and sadness I'd been feeling since Mum told me spilt over like an erupting volcano. I was on my feet. All my thoughts of reasoning with him had flown out the window.

'Liar. You're a liar. You've been lying to us – to Mum and me – all this time. I'll never forgive you. And you can't be both – you can't be my dad and –' I hesitated. I didn't want to say the name – 'and *Dawn*.' The word felt like poison in my mouth. 'It's one or the other.'

Dad – Dawn – was on his feet too.

'People change. I've changed. But the changes are with my body, not my heart. I'll always love you, both of you. And I'm sorry if this hurts you—'

'*If* it hurts?!' I spat the words at him. Her. 'What do you mean, *if*? It's like being in a bad dream that's going to last for the rest of my life. You're not my dad any more. I'll never see you or even think about you again!'

The tears spilt over.

I stumbled towards the door, knocking over the Indian table. The photo crashed on to the ground and the glass cracked and fell away in sharp shards, leaving the picture of our happy family looking like someone had shot a bullet through it.

Dad reached towards me.

'Dan, please!'

'No. Leave me alone! You're selfish and I wish you were dead. From now on, you're dead to me.'

I pulled the door open and was outside in less than a second.

Snow had started to fall. The flakes felt like a woman's cold fingers, stroking my skin. Maybe those fingers had red nails, like Dad's.

The thought made me gag. I pulled my coat around me and ran off into the darkness.

Chapter 15

When I got home, I told Mum that I'd gone to see Dad. She already knew. He must have rung her as soon as I'd left.

'He . . . she told me you were upset. What did you expect, Dan? You should have waited. It would have been easier with me there.'

'I wanted to see him by myself. To reason with him. But I couldn't. When I saw him, all plucked and covered in make-up, I forgot what I wanted to say. I just had to get out of there . . .'

'Come again. With me. Give it a few days,' she said. 'Maybe you'll feel different now you know what to expect.'

'Never! I don't want to see him again. Ever.'

She sighed and rubbed her temples, like she had a headache.

'You know, don't you, that we either accept Dawn or we cut her out of our lives. There's no other way!'

I jumped to my feet.

'Then I'm cutting him out of my life,' I yelled, before storming upstairs.

She didn't follow me.

Two crappy days later, we were in Biology. Naomi was sitting with some of her new buddies and I was paired up with Ashley Wicks, whose normal partner was off sick. I don't mind Ashley, but he doesn't like science and always mucks around which annoys me. If he fooled around in any other subject I'd be fine with it, but not Biology.

We were doing an experiment with a bunch of test tubes in a rack. Unusual, but it was pretty cool. While we were doing it, Mr Bennet got the lab assistant to hand back our exercise books. He didn't look at me in particular or say anything and I thought, *yes! I've got away with ruining my homework*. He must have been busy with the rugby and drinking at the weekend.

The experiment went well, in spite of Ashley's attempts to mess it up, and for a while I forgot everything apart from the blue stab of flame from the Bunsen burner and the weird smells and changing colours coming from the liquids bubbling in the test tube racks. I couldn't help noticing that Naomi was struggling with her experiment. It must have been because she'd chosen to do it with Emma Renfield, who's nice but not interested, rather than me. That would teach her.

The lesson was coming to an end and Mr Bennet made a point of saying well done to Ashley and me. Most of the other pairs' experiments had failed, too.

'Homework for this week is to write up your experiment and draw a diagram showing how it worked. If it didn't work – which will be most of you – write what you think *should* have happened. Or ask Dan and Ashley to explain what happened in theirs.' Mr Bennet was busy writing it up on the whiteboard.

We all jotted it down in our homework diaries and were heading for the door when Mr Bennet called out:

'That reminds me. I need a word with Dan Yates. Stay behind, will you Dan? The rest of you – see you next lesson.'

My heart sank.

The rest of the class filed out. As she passed me, Naomi knocked my shoulder and when I looked at her, she opened her eyes wide and nodded at the same time. She didn't say anything, and I didn't know what she was trying to make me understand. I just looked away and prepared myself for trouble. I noticed that Josh and Kyra were walking out really slowly, hoping to hear me getting a telling off, but Mr Bennet told Josh to hurry up and shut the door behind him and waited until he'd done it.

Then he sat on his desk and kicked his legs backwards and forwards and looked at me.

'Dan. Talk to me.'

'What about, sir?'

'You know what about. You ruined your homework, deliberately and in a way that I find quite worrying. There's something bothering you. No, don't shake your head at me. When my best pupil starts defacing their homework and I hear about all the other uncharacteristic things he was up to last week, alarm bells start ringing. What's up?'

I liked Mr Bennet and, as a Biology teacher, he should understand all about transsexuals and stuff like that. But could I trust him? What if he told someone? Just one other person? And that someone told someone else? And that someone else told two of their friends, and so on and so on? It would take about a day for the whole school to know that my dad was a freak. I'd already told the only person in school I trusted – Naomi. Even though we'd fallen out, I wasn't worried that she'd split on me.

That made me think about how things had changed in the time since Dad left. Before then, I'd never had to think too much about what came out of my mouth. I'd never needed to keep secrets, or wanted to. Now it seemed like my whole life was turning into one ginormous secret. I wondered if I'd spend the rest of my life worrying about who knew and who I could trust and trying to think up lies and excuses in advance, just in case. Dad had made me the keeper of a secret I didn't want in the first place, and I hated it.

Mr Bennet must have been watching my face closely, because just as I opened my mouth to come out with some lame lie, he held up one hand.

'Don't, Dan. You've got a very open face and I can see what's going through your mind.' He thought for a second and he then said: 'I'm not going to report this. From what I hear from Mr Hodges and Mrs Llewellyn, you're in enough trouble as it is. But I'm going to ask this of you – come to me when you're ready to talk. Or if you're getting the urge to do something else out of character. I know there's something going on, and I can tell it's pretty serious. Just come and find me when you're ready and try and keep out of trouble until then. Don't muck up. Yes?'

Suddenly I wanted to tell him something, to reward him for not splitting on me. But I wouldn't tell him the truth. I would keep to what I'd said to Dad as I left his flat. It was true on one level, anyway.

I took a deep breath.

'Actually, sir, it's my dad. He's dead.'

Chapter 16

He believed me. For about ten seconds. And then I watched as the expression on his face changed from concern to doubt.

'I hate to doubt you, Dan. And if that's true, I'm really, really sorry. But you've got to see it from my point of view. No one at school knows anything about this, and that's strange. Normally, things like that get around fast. So, I'll need to check this out. I'll be the first to apologise for doubting you if—'

In my head, I finished the sentence for him. *If you're not lying.* Well, I wasn't, not really. Dad *was* dead, or as good as. When someone died, you never saw them again, and I'd never see Dad again, at least not the Dad I knew and loved. In his place there was this red-nailed freak called Dawn.

I looked into Mr Bennet's frowning face and opened my mouth, but I didn't know what to say. What was happening to me? I was turning into a liar, I'd lost my best friend and my life was falling apart. If I carried on like this, I'd end up being chucked out of school and then I'd never be a vet.

'I'm sorry,' I mumbled and turned and ran off. I half expected to hear him yelling after me to come back, but he didn't.

I ran out of the science department and past reception, where Mrs Chaudri was answering about ten phones at once, over the soggy playing field and I didn't stop until I was on the road into town.

What I wanted, more than anything, was to find Naomi and tell her what I'd said. She'd understand why but she'd tell me off anyway for being a prat and somehow things wouldn't seem so bad. But I couldn't do that. Naomi was having fun with her new friends and wouldn't be interested in what I had to say. I wondered if I should apologise to her, but it didn't seem right. *She* had upset *me*, not the other way round, and anyway, she'd probably just laugh and tell me to leave her alone.

I hunched my shoulders and turned up the collar of my blazer. It was freezing, and my tears felt like they were turning to ice on my face. I decided that going back to school would be pointless, so I dug my hands into my trouser pockets and walked towards the shops.

Town was busier than usual. People were buying presents and rushing around like Christmas was the next day, not in three weeks' time. I watched them and wondered if they knew how stupid they looked, hurrying and frowning and swinging bags full of stuff that no one really wanted. Usually I loved Christmas, but not now. Christmas was another thing that Dad had destroyed for me.

I saw our neighbour, Mrs Pollard, again. She'd been about to cross the road near the discount shop but she saw me walking towards her and stopped. I wondered if she was going to ask me what had happened to Dad. Or why I wasn't in school. I pretended I hadn't seen her and that I'd spotted something really great in the window of the discount shop. I swerved across the road and into the shop before she had the chance to call out to me or wave or something.

Inside there was a tall display of DVDs that no one had heard of and that no one wanted to buy. I peeped around the corner of it. Oh hell! Mrs Pollard was crossing the road, too. She must be determined to pin me down. I remembered a scene in a James Bond film where Bond is being chased by the villain and the villain follows him into a shop and thinks he's got him cornered. But Bond waits until the bad guy dashes into the shop and he runs out another door at exactly the same moment and the baddie doesn't know he's gone and spends ages looking for him behind perfume counters and displays of tights. Actually, it might have been an episode of *Mr Bean*, not a Bond film. It doesn't sound spectacular enough for that. But anyway, I thought I'd do the same thing.

It worked. I don't know how many hours Mrs Pollard spent in there, pouncing behind stacks of nearly-out-of-date biscuits and rummaging in the wire bins of cheap cat toys, just in case I was hiding in the bottom. I hope it was a long time.

I rushed back into the street, turning behind me to check that Mrs P wasn't on my trail, and went *SMACK!* Straight into someone.

They staggered around like they were unsteady in their shoes and then toppled to the ground, spilling a carrier bag of supermarket ready meals on to the pavement.

'I'm really sorry!' I began scrabbling around, picking up the ready meals and stuffing them back into the carrier bag without looking at who I'd knocked over.

It wasn't until I'd shoved the final one back that I looked up to see who I'd cannoned into.

It was the Lady Man, struggling to stand up.

Chapter 17

'Oh,' I said, and then didn't know what else to say. The Lady Man looked cross and sad at the same time, under his too heavy make-up. He was wearing a purple jumper with a high frilly collar that made the top of his neck look thick, and a checked skirt and a coat in another kind of check that clashed with the skirt. On his legs, which looked more like a footballer's than a woman's, he wore those horrible, orangey brown tights like my gran used to wear. I'd asked her about them once and she said the colour was called Natural Tan and laughed when I said that I thought a better name would be Unnatural Fake Tan. On his feet were brown ankle boots with thin, spiky heels. They must have been really hard to walk in.

I looked at him and he looked at me and neither of us seemed to know what to say.

'Did you do that on purpose?' he asked eventually, in a gentle voice that could have belonged to a man or a woman.

I gaped at him.

'No! Of course not.'

'Hidden your mates around the corner, where they can have a good laugh?'

'No. I wouldn't do that. It was an accident.'

The Lady Man folded his arms.

'Hmmm. Well, all I can say is, Cherrington must be the most accident-prone place in the country. People seem to have "accidents" –' he made air speech marks with his fingers – 'about three times a day. And they always involve me! Usually, they just shove into me or stick out a foot to trip me up. This is the first time the assault has been so blatant.'

Assault! I didn't know what blatant meant, but I knew what assault was. It was hurting someone deliberately. You could go to prison for it.

'No. I wouldn't! I didn't! It was an accident. I was trying to escape from my next-door neighbour. Honestly.'

The Lady Man was dusting down his skirt and coat. Then he picked up his carrier bag. One of the handles had broken in the accident and half of the ready meals fell out on to the pavement again.

'Look what you've done! You can jolly well help me to get these home!'

Help the Lady Man? No way on Earth. I was racking my brain for some excuse when I remembered what Kim had said about him being brave and getting bullied a lot. That must be the 'accidents' he talked about.

'Do you live far away?' I asked.

I thought I saw a twinkle in his eyes.

'Barstock. It's quite a long way, but it won't take more than a couple of hours on the bus . . .'

Two hours with the Lady Man? What if I was seen with him? And then two hours to get home again. And what about bus fare?

'Oh, but I can't. I'm due at . . .' I couldn't think of where I could be expected. I shut up and looked at him.

He looked back at me straight-faced for about half a year and then he did something I wasn't expecting.

He smiled.

'Relax, kid. I'm just pulling your leg. I live a few streets away. I really could do with a hand with this shopping, if you're not too ashamed of being seen with me?' He lifted his plucked eyebrows.

Of course I was ashamed to be seen with him. Who wouldn't be? But somehow, I looked into the Lady Man's twinkling eyes and I couldn't say that.

'No, no, it's OK.' I started picking up the shopping again. Ready meals for one. How sad. I wondered if Dad was eating them too? Then I added, 'But I'm not coming in or anything,' just in case he was a paedophile as well as a freak.

'Nobody's asking you!' the Lady Man said, with another twinkle. I think that he must have realised what I was thinking. I don't know how. Maybe it was my face giving me away again, like it had with Mr Bennet.

We walked in silence and I kept my eyes firmly on the pavement, in case I passed anyone I knew. My cat Nelson does this thing when he goes to the vet. He hides his head under my arm, thinking that if he can't see the vet, the vet can't see him. I guess I'd got the idea from him.

After a few minutes, the shoppers thinned out and I thought it was safe to ask a question.

'What's your name?'

'Laura,' he said. I risked a quick glance up at his face and he caught me doing it. 'Or do you mean my old name?'

'Both, I guess,' I mumbled, feeling stupid.

'My old name was Leslie. Les. I suppose I could have kept the old name and just changed the spelling – L-E-S-L-E-Y instead of L-E-S-L-I-E – but it wouldn't have felt like a new beginning then. And it would have felt like I was cheating.'

I could understand that, sort of. I'm sure if I was going to turn my life upside down, I would want a different name to do it with. Maybe Zane or Zack. It would be hard not to be cool with a name that started with Z.

'Why do you want to be a woman?' Maybe with Les I could ask that question and stand to listen to the answer.

Les looked suddenly fierce.

'I *AM* a woman in here,' he thumped his heart. 'And I can't go through life any longer pretending that I'm not. I've only got one life and I don't want to waste it living a lie. When I've lived like this for a while, it will prove that I'm really serious about being a woman and I'll be able to have the ops to make it happen.' He peered down at me. I think he was trying to see if I understood.

For some reason I started thinking about the Jungle Book. Mowgli gets brought up by a wolf pack, which must be really cool as long as you don't mind raw meat, but underneath he's a human and he needs to live as one. I wondered how he'd feel if he'd carried on living as a wolf. In the end it would have made him unhappy, especially when it came to finding a girlfriend and stuff like that.

'I think I get what you're saying,' I said. 'Sort of. Do you have a family?'

He looked sad then.

'Had. I had a family. They don't want to know me now.'

'Doesn't that make you want to give all this up? You could go back to them, maybe. Start again.'

Les gave a deep sigh.

'If only it was that easy. I think about doing that sometimes but I know that the happiness of doing it would be temporary. Then I'd do this again because I just *have* to, and the heartbreak would start all over again. Not just mine. My wife's. My kids'. So it's better to stick it out . . . I see my kids sometimes, from a distance. They look OK . . .'

I thought about that. Poor Les. Unhappy with his family and unhappy without them. What kind of a choice was that? Was it the same with Dad?

'I'm sorry,' I mumbled. 'That it's so hard for you.'

'Thanks, kid.' He looked down at me. 'It's good to talk to you. A nice change . . . What's your name?'

I told him.

'Well, Dan, you sound genuinely interested and I appreciate that. I hope we'll bump into each other again sometime. Not literally though, next time! This is where I live . . .'

Les's house looked depressing. It was in Prince Albert Street, in the oldest part of town, in the middle of a terrace. It needed painting. It had no front garden and cars and vans were parked half on the pavement, making it too narrow for two people to walk together comfortably.

'Maybe,' I said. And then, because I felt like I should say something more, I added: 'Look out on the slippery pavements with those wobbly boots of yours. It sounds like you have enough accidents as it is!'

Les gave a little laugh.

I was glad about that. His life seemed sad and I'd made him happy for a minute.

'See you,' I said, and ran back to the centre of town.

Chapter 18

I don't know why, but talking with Les made me feel a bit better about life and I started to think about Naomi. I missed her a lot and looking back on what she'd said about playing Prince Charming, I could see that she hadn't done it to upset me – just the opposite, probably. The Dad situation was making me ultra-sensitive and maybe I'd overreacted a tiny bit.

I texted her: *Want 2 meet up after skool? Sorry about last week.*☺ And waited for her to reply. She wouldn't be long. She wasn't the type to hold grudges.

Half an hour later, I'd heard nothing so I texted her again: *Not mad at me r u?*

Nothing. She must be busy. Maybe she was rehearsing and couldn't look at her phone. Another half an hour went by. I decided to give it one more go. *U not my pal any more?*☹

Still nothing, and she must have had time to look by now. I knew Naomi. The only time she wasn't checking her phone was when she was asleep. Her mum liked to joke that she might as well have it grafted to her hand. My good mood went up in smoke. That was it. I'd lost my best friend and it was my own stupid fault.

I hunched my shoulders and trudged home.

And walked straight into an argument.

I heard the voices before I'd even opened the garden gate. Three of them: Mum's, Dad's and Grandad's. Just what I needed. I thought about keeping on walking. I could go to Burger King and drink a Coke or something until they'd sorted themselves out, or maybe stay out till really late to teach them a lesson, but it was cold so I headed inside.

'—then you're no son of mine!' Grandad was yelling.

'Keep your voice down. The neighbours will hear,' Mum hissed.

'Sod the neighbours! Who cares if they hear? It's none of their flaming business,' Dad said.

'You're ruining your life. And not just yours. Joanne's and Dan's as well! Your mother will be turning in her grave.'

I walked into living room and stood just inside the door. Mum was hunched up on the sofa, crying again. I wondered how many tears a human being could cry? Did you reach a million or something and then you ran out? Mum must be nearing that stage by now. Her tear ducts must be working overtime.

Dad and Grandad were facing each other. Grandad was sticking his chin out like an angry chimp. He was poking Dad in the arm.

Dad was facing him. Normally he was about the same height as Grandad but he was wearing boots with heels and they made him a bit taller. Even though he was taller, he looked scared. Grandad's pretty fierce when he gets going. It made me feel sorry for Dad. He never loses his temper and he didn't now, even with Grandad yelling at him.

They were too busy arguing to notice me.

'Actually, Dad, you're wrong. Mum would be OK with it. Do you want to know why I'm so sure? I promised never to tell you but it can't matter now. She knew. About my other life. She found me trying on a dress of hers when I was thirteen. She didn't understand, but she didn't condemn me either, said it was something I would probably grow out of and it was harming no one. So you can't use Mum to back up your Stone-Age ideas!'

Grandad took a step back. His face went as pale as a sheet. I knew how he was feeling.

Gran *knew?* That was something I'd have to think about later. Right now, I needed to stop all the shouting and hating.

I stepped forward.

'STOP!' I yelled. 'You're just making things worse.'

Everyone turned to look at me.

'I'll decide if my life's ruined, no one else,' I continued. 'You're all too angry to sort anything out at the moment. You need to go into separate rooms or something till you calm down.'

There was silence.

'You should be ashamed of yourselves. You sound

like a pack of little kids having an argument in the playground. You're supposed to be *grown-ups*!'

Dad gave a shaky laugh.

'You're right, Dan . . . Dad, let's talk about this another time, if we have to. Jo, shall we meet for a chat in a day or two? Maybe have a coffee? Or I'll come here if you don't want to be seen with me.' His pink painted lips twisted. 'I'll go now.'

He picked up his mac, which was thrown over a chair, and started to put it on.

'You should put up the Christmas tree,' he said to Mum as he turned to the door. 'You know how much you love doing that.' He looked at me. 'Dan, I hope I'll see you soon. You know where I am. Or I'll meet you anywhere you want.'

Meet him? In public? That just wasn't going to happen.

I didn't say anything but he must have read my mind. He turned and left without another word.

Chapter 19

The next day at school, I suppose you could say that the poop hit the fan.

As soon as I walked past reception and saw Mrs Chaudri frowning at me, I knew that I was in trouble.

I thought about turning round and hiding in town, but I was getting fed up of that. Bunking off wasn't all it was cracked up to be and every time I did it, something seemed to go wrong that just made things worse.

The Hedgehog had got to class early and I wondered later if he'd made the effort just to make the most of his chance to humiliate me. He had his head down, reading a note, when I walked in and for a few seconds, while I walked past Naomi, who was too busy chatting with Kyra McGee to notice me, and on to my new seat next to Hannah Sullivan, who looked pleased, as if I'd chosen her on purpose or something, I thought it was going to be OK.

Then the Hedgehog put down the note he was

frowning over, and looked up. Straight at me.

'Dan Yates! This really isn't your term, is it?'

That made Naomi's head swivel my way.

My guts churned but I did my best to hide it.

'Why? What have I done now, sir?'

'Short of bank robbery, there doesn't seem to be much that you haven't done! Mrs Llewellyn's waiting for you. Try not to add to the tally of your misdemeanours before you get there, will you?'

The whole class sniggered. Well, nearly the whole class. Naomi didn't, and neither did Hannah Sullivan. She looked sad and tried to squeeze my hand but I pulled it away. I didn't want her getting ideas.

As I made my way to the door, I made a point of not looking Naomi's way.

The Hedgehog hadn't finished yet.

'I've been reading in the local paper that there's a mini crime wave in Cherrington. Anything to do with you?'

To be honest, I could feel tears stinging my eyes by then, but I wasn't going to show myself up so I just ignored him and walked out.

The walk to Mrs Llewellyn's office seemed really long, but it was still over too soon. All the way there I was thinking: *this is it. You're gonna get expelled. You'll never be a vet. You'll be an outcast and have to join the Foreign Legion.* I saw a film where that happened and I knew that the Foreign Legion wouldn't be fun, despite its exciting image. It wasn't all camel rides. Sometimes, your enemies buried you up to your neck in the sand

and left to you to dry out, like a grounded jellyfish.

'I'll ring through to say you're here. Just sit outside her office and she'll come out and get you when she's ready,' Mrs Chaudri said. She gave me a sad-looking smile that made me feel even worse.

There's a waiting area outside Mrs Llewellyn's office. It's just a corridor, really, with four chairs covered with itchy blue material and a cabinet with a few cups and trophies and photos in. The walls are covered with what Mrs Llewellyn calls 'the best art from our talented pupils', although if you ask me that doesn't say much for the not-so-good art from the less talented ones. There's a portrait of the Queen that looks like Simon Cowell in a grey wig, and the picture of the *Star Wars* stormtrooper being eaten by wolves is just plain weird. I had a long time to examine them, because I was sitting there, trying to keep still in one of the itchy chairs, for a long time. I could hear murmurs inside Mrs Llewellyn's office. There was another woman in there with her. I strained my ears trying to hear what they were saying, but I couldn't.

At last, the door opened and Mrs Llewellyn's head appeared round it.

'Come in, Dan,' she said.

I got up and walked in like I was going to a ten-hour exam on a subject I'd never even studied. And stopped dead, just inside the door.

Mum was there, sitting in a green armchair that looked about a hundred years old.

'Oh,' I said, like an idiot.

Mum's face was puffy, but at least she wasn't crying. Maybe she'd reached that million tear-mark and run dry.

'Hi, Dan,' she said. She gave me a little smile.

'Hi, Mum,' I managed.

'Sit down, Dan,' Mrs Llewellyn said.

I went to sit in the orange chair where the bad kids sit, but Mrs Llewellyn put up one hand.

'You don't need to sit there, Dan. Take the seat next to your mum.'

I wasn't expecting that. I hurried over and sat down in the other hundred-year-old green armchair.

'I wish you'd told me,' Mrs Llewellyn said. 'About your father.'

'I'm sorry . . . It's hard to talk about.'

'Yes. It must be. But thank heaven your mum came in to talk to me before anything else happened. There are two things I want to say to you, Dan. The first is that you can talk to us. You won't shock us. What your dad is doing – undergoing gender reassignment – is increasingly common and you won't be telling us anything that we haven't been trained to handle. So, next time you get the urge to bunk off, or to punch someone for saying something that they don't know will hurt you, come and see me. Or Mr Bennet. Or Mr Hodges. We'll listen and understand. And keep you out of trouble.'

'Mr *Hodges*?' The words came out before I could stop them. I couldn't imagine the Hedgehog being understanding about anything.

Mrs Llewellyn smiled.

'Yes, Mr Hodges. He's actually the best qualified of all of us when it comes to student counselling.'

'But he's—'

'I know he can appear a little – brusque – at times, but his bark is worse than his bite. Try him sometime. You'll be surprised.'

I needed to think about that, so I just said OK.

'Thank you,' Mum said to Mrs Llewellyn. 'As you know, Dan's being counselled out of school, but that's more to do with the practical side of – of – changing sex. Having someone he knows he can go to and talk about – the emotional side of things – will be a big help.'

Hmph, I thought. I could deal with my own emotions without needing help from the Hedgehog, but I nodded anyway.

'What's the other thing, Miss?'

Mrs Llewellyn smiled.

'I just wanted to tell you something that not many people know. I can't give you any details for obvious reasons, but I thought it might be useful for you to know that you're not the only pupil here with a parent in similar circumstances. As I said, it's more common than people realise.'

What? Someone else at Cherry High School had a Lady Man dad? Or a Man Lady mum? That was something I'd never considered. Who was it? How did they hide it? Did they get bullied? I started running through everyone I knew at school, but I couldn't work out who it could be. No one else I knew was bunking off and ruining their homework and getting in trouble every day. Maybe they'd learnt to deal with it.

'Who? Is it their mum or their dad?'

'Dan, you don't expect me to answer that question. It's highly confidential. But I hope you'll take comfort in knowing that you're not alone. And actually, the parent in question finished the treatment a good two years ago, and nobody gives the child any trouble about it, if that's worrying you. We'll be just as careful with your information. Rest assured.'

Rest. It seemed to me like I hadn't had much rest lately. It sounded good. I missed it.

Mrs Llewellyn got to her feet.

'I'll make sure that everyone who needs to know *does* know. No one will treat you differently. We'll just understand a bit better, if something goes wrong . . . Off to your first lesson now. And Dan? Try and make it a good day!'

Chapter 20

It wasn't a bad day, after that. We had swimming which I really like, even though you come out smelling like toilet cleaner, and Physics where we split light with prisms. Making your own personal rainbow was pretty cool, even without Naomi to enjoy it with. She was partnered with Emma Renfield again. I suppose she must enjoy doing all the work, while Emma hides her phone under the table and spends the lesson texting someone or other.

Apart from the cool lessons, I felt better now that Mrs Llewellyn knew what was happening. I couldn't really explain why, but it made me feel protected. I still couldn't imagine talking to Sarcasmo if I had any more problems, though.

I was a little late for afternoon register because I needed the toilet just as the bell rang and I hurried into our form room expecting him to have a go at me.

'Sorry, sir. Call of nature,' I said. That wasn't one of Grandad's sayings. I don't know where I'd heard it, but anything to do with nature was cool and I liked the idea that our bodies were doing what they were designed to do.

I waited for the sarcasm to flow.

But he actually smiled at me.

'OK, Dan. Try not to make a habit of it.'

That was it. The rest of the class looked as shocked as I must have. When I took my seat by Hannah, I felt relieved. Mrs Llewellyn must have told him what was happening. I was glad that my teachers had started to understand me again. Maybe my life wasn't ruined and I would still be able to be a vet.

I looked at Naomi but she was deep in conversation with Ashley Wicks, laughing at whatever he was saying like it was the funniest thing she'd ever heard. I felt my good mood dissolve a little bit.

There were rehearsals for the pantomime that evening, and I went along to find out what I would need to do behind the stage. Mr Bennet was there, and when I walked in he stopped talking to Kyra McGee and came over to me.

'Glad you opened up, Dan. Well done,' he said in a quiet voice. That was it, but it made me feel like I'd done something amazing instead of just admitting that things were tough to the head teacher.

Naomi was there but she wasn't rehearsing her part. Instead it was the chorus, singing a song about wishing they had bigger parts in the play, which was actually quite clever, when I thought about it.

I didn't have to see much of Naomi because Mr

Bennet took me and the other volunteers backstage, checking out the scenery and the props (things that you put on the stage to make it look more realistic). That was pretty interesting, especially when Raj in Year 9 got hold of the plastic skull that the sixth formers had been using for some Shakespeare project and chased Sophie Mason outside with it. She's got a good pair of lungs. And then Mr Bennet said it wasn't plastic at all, it was REAL and then Sophie screamed even louder until the Hedgehog, who was doing his Steven Spielberg bit, yelled at her to shut up. I decided that being a stage hand was going to be fun.

When the rehearsal finished, I thought about having one more try at making up with Naomi. I really missed her. And, if I was honest with myself, I needed her – especially at the moment. I needed to talk to her and listen to what she had to say and to know that she was on my side. Maybe I could ask her if she wanted to go into town. But by the time we'd put all the props away so that the stage could be used for Assembly the next day, and Mr Bennet had got Raj to hand over the skull and persuaded Sophie to come out of the cupboard she was hiding in, Naomi had already left.

I ran out of the hall, thinking that I could catch up with her if she wasn't too far ahead, but she was walking with Ashley and Kyra and Josh, and I knew that I couldn't talk to her in front of that crowd. They would snigger and make fun of me and I'd want to crawl under the nearest rock and hide. And if Naomi sniggered too, that would just about finish me off.

Still, I thought I'd go into town anyway. Not that I was going to follow Naomi or anything. I just didn't want to go home yet. And we just happened to going the same way and I'd already decided to take the short cut through the park, even before I saw Naomi and co heading in that direction.

It was quite dark in the park, even though there are lamp posts about every twenty metres. Naomi and the others were quite a long way in front of me but I could see their dark shapes shoving at each other as they walked. I could hear them, too. Josh was practising his solo from the pantomime, giving it a load of wobbly notes that I guess he thought sounded professional. I thought he sounded like a prat. A few people passed me, hurrying home from work. Or maybe they were trying to get away from Josh's singing.

I was going past the flowerbeds, thinking that Baby Jesus looked even worse than the last time now that the yellow flowers that made up his halo had died. He looked like he was wearing a brown crash helmet. Suddenly I heard some noises I didn't like: raised voices and scuffling. I wondered if someone was in trouble. Then I heard a thud and a little cry and I knew for definite that someone needed help. I stood and listened, thinking about what the Hedgehog had said earlier about a mini crime wave in Cherrington. Maybe this was part of it. Maybe someone was being mugged.

I turned in a circle, trying to work out where the noise was coming from. As I swung round, I saw that Naomi and her pals had stopped too. They had gone quiet. Even Josh had shut up. They must have heard the noises as well.

I'd just worked out that they were coming from the old bandstand, about a hundred metres ahead and to my left, when a gust of wind carried some words to me.

'Pathetic freak . . . what's in your handbag, Lady Man? Let's get his wig off him . . .'

My heart seemed to stop.

Oh no! *Dad!* Some bullies were hassling him. What if they wanted to hurt him?

I was about to sprint towards him when I had another thought. Why should I help? If he got beaten up, he only had himself to blame. Then I thought maybe this would be what he needed to show him that what he was doing was stupid. Maybe it would change his mind. Maybe it would make him come home and start being David again.

Then I heard a scared cry and some more scuffling.

That was enough. Dad was in trouble and if I didn't help him, no one would. What if the bullies had knives? What if they really hated transsexuals and had decided to kill one?

'I'm coming!' I yelled.

I broke into a run.

As I hurtled past Naomi and the others, Josh called out to me.

'Don't bother. It's only the Lady Man.'

I didn't reply. It wasn't worth it. But as I passed them I thought that Naomi's eyes were wide open with concern.

'Huh. One freak helping another one . . .' Josh said.

'Josh, get—' I heard Naomi say, but I was already too far away to hear any more. I was already wondering what on earth I could do to help. One kid couldn't do much. But I had to try.

I began to make out their shapes in the gloom. There were four: three male and one female. As I got closer, I saw that the three males were young, maybe sixth formers. They wore jeans and puffer jackets that they didn't do up. Maybe they thought they were too cool to keep warm. Two of them were waving cans of lager around. You could smell the sour booze on them. It was a lot worse than Mum's wine. One of them grabbed at Dad's long hair.

Dad reached up to protect his hair, but the bully gave him a shove and he staggered backwards, leaving his hair in the bully's hand. The bully gave a whoop of excitement. Dad looked like he'd been scalped. It made my heart twist with shame and pity.

I couldn't bear it. '*Oi! Leave her alone!*' I yelled the words as loud as I could. Maybe it would startle them into running off.

By now I was close enough to see things more clearly. The woman was wearing a checked coat over a dress or skirt and ankle boots with spiky heels. It wasn't Dad, it was Laura! I saw that her real hair was short and messed up from wearing the wig. It looked a bit like baby's hair.

Everyone stopped what they were doing and looked at me.

'*Dan?*' Laura said. 'Keep out of this.' She sounded annoyed. Or maybe worried.

The bully with her wig waved it in front of me.

'Yeah, *Dan*. You'd better run back to the kiddie swings where you belong.' His voice was slurred.

When I realised that it wasn't Dad being attacked I felt relieved for a second, but now the anger was back, surging around inside my body. I guess it was adrenalin. Fight or flight, like with predators and prey in the jungle. Well, I wasn't going to flee and leave the bullies to do horrible things to someone who didn't deserve it. Someone who seemed quite nice.

'No! Leave her alone. Or I'll—'

The bully dropped Laura's wig on the floor and curled his hands into fists.

'Or you'll what? What you gonna do, *Dan?*'

Chapter 21

The bully lumbered towards me like a silverback gorilla seeing off competitors. I saw Laura's eyes, wide open with fear. She made a movement towards me but one of the bullies grabbed her and held her back.

The bully who was coming for me raised his fists. The other one – the one who wasn't holding Laura back – moved towards me too, grinning. I looked up into his face. He had a load of red spots around his mouth. I remember thinking, *great, I'm gonna get beaten up by someone with a face like a pizza.*

I raised my fists like Sherlock Holmes had done in a movie I'd seen, but I dropped them again. Who was I trying to kid? I was about to get into a fight with two *men*, or nearly men, who were at least six inches taller than me and much heavier. I was going to get hurt. I looked behind me, thinking for a second that I should run away, but I couldn't do that. If I did, Laura would get beaten up and they would be even more vicious with her than they would with me. They hated her.

And then there was a flash of bright light in the gloom.

'Smile for the camera!' Naomi's voice called out. 'You're gonna be on *Crimewatch*!'

'Wha—?' The bully stopped and swung round. We all did.

Naomi was standing there with her phone aimed at us.

'I've rung the police. They'll be here any minute. I think I'll put the video on Facebook. I'm sure loads of people would like to see you four heroes beating up a woman and a kid.' She raised her eyebrows and gave them her most sarcastic smile. I knew that smile. It made you feel tiny and kind of exposed at the same time – like the dead frogs we had to dissect in Biology. She must have been scared, but she didn't let it show.

The bully holding Laura's arms let go of them.

'That's not a woman. It's a freak! He's gay!' he stuttered.

Laura rushed to pick up her wig and jammed it back on her head. It was wonky but she looked a lot better. More like herself.

'When it comes to freaks, I don't think you're much of a judge,' she said, adjusting her hair. 'Try looking in the mirror sometime.'

Somewhere in the distance there was a police siren, coming closer.

'They're nearly here,' Naomi said, looking over her shoulder. 'Better run.'

They did.

The three of us – Naomi and Laura and me – stood there for a few seconds, just looking at each other. I felt sick and I think maybe they did, too. Then Laura spoke.

'Thanks. You shouldn't have done it – you know that, don't you? It could have turned out very differently. But – thank you. So much.'

She grabbed my hand and shook it. Really shook it, like she was pumping up a bike tyre with a hand pump. Then she did the same to Naomi.

'Do you want us to walk with you?' I asked Laura.

She gave a shaky little laugh. 'If you're going my way, I wouldn't say no. Thanks again, Dan and . . . ?' She raised her eyebrows at Naomi.

'This is Naomi. My best friend,' I said, glad that it was true again.

We walked her all the way back to Prince Albert Street, chatting about *Crimewatch* and Christmas – anything except the bullies – and what else they might have done. When Laura opened her door, she gave us a smile that almost cracked her lipstick.

'Well, this is me. Thanks again, both of you. Drop by any time . . .' She turned to go in, but then she stopped and turned back, frowning. 'We should have waited for the police, I suppose . . . I wasn't thinking straight . . .'

Naomi grinned.

'I didn't really call the police. There wasn't time . . . That siren was pure coincidence. But someone up there must be looking out for us.' She nodded skywards.

We all laughed and I thought how amazing Naomi was, and how my life was so much better with her in it.

We started walking back towards town.

'Did you think it was your Dad?' Naomi asked me, after a bit.

'Yeah. Laura's like her. I met her yesterday. She's OK, considering.'

Naomi nodded.

'What happened to Josh and the others?' I asked.

'I don't know and I don't care. Ran off like a bunch of chickens, I expect. I told Josh to get lost when he called you a freak. We won't be hanging out together any more.'

That sounded good to me.

'I'm sorry. For getting upset with you. About the pantomime. You weren't doing anything wrong, I just wasn't seeing things properly,' I said.

'I know. It's OK,' Naomi threaded one of her arms through mine and we matched paces.

'But why didn't you answer my texts? I've been trying to apologise and you blanked me totally. I thought you hated me.'

She waved her phone at me.

'I dropped this down the loo. Had to get it mended. I only picked it up half an hour ago. The first thing I saw was your messages. I've replied but I don't think you've seen it yet.'

That explained everything. Relief washed over me.

'Come on. Fries and Coke on me!'

We sat in the warmth of the Burger Hut, surrounded by the familiar smells of frying food and the familiar sounds of people chatting about nothing very interesting, and I thought that maybe things were looking up. My teachers were on my side, I was enjoying being a stage hand, Naomi and me had made up and we'd rescued someone from drunken bullies. We were heroes!

We looked across to the square, where the Christmas tree was twinkling. There was an orchestra beneath it, playing Christmas songs. I couldn't see who they were but they weren't very good. Maybe it was a primary school orchestra. They needed to practise more. Unless there really was a thrash metal version of 'Away in a Manger'.

I grinned at Naomi and thought that maybe Christmas wouldn't be a complete disaster, after all.

Chapter 22

A day or so after, I asked Naomi to go Christmas shopping after school. I wanted to buy her a present but I didn't really have much idea what she'd like. I remembered that she didn't seem very impressed with the bobble hat I'd given her for her thirteenth birthday in June. This time, I wanted to get it right.

When she said she was busy and could we do it another night, I was a bit miffed. It was late-night Christmas shopping, and there would be toffee apples and hot dogs and brass bands and a Christmas market selling things like socks from Peru and candles shaped like unicorns. There was bound to be something there that she liked.

I wanted to ask her where she needed to go that was more important, but I decided not to. If she wanted me to know, she'd have told me.

In the end, I went with Mum. I saw Josh Jacobs over the other side of the market and I was worried for a second. I thought he'd laugh at me for being with my mum, but then I noticed that he was with both of his parents and I relaxed. His dad is pretty embarrassing. He wears brown and yellow checked trousers and a red scarf, and when he laughs, he sounds like a braying donkey. He reminds me of Rupert the Bear.

Mum and me looked around the stalls and Mum bought a pair of Peruvian knitted leg warmers and some homemade jam and chutney. She looked happy to be out and doing something normal like Christmas shopping, so I was glad we'd come. I found a stall selling friendship bracelets with beads and shells woven into them and I decided that Naomi would love them, so I bought her a red, yellow and blue one. She always likes bright colours.

We listened to the brass band playing 'While Shepherds Watched their Flocks by Night' and that made me sad for a while. Dad always insists that the words are *When shepherds washed their socks by night*, and we all laugh, even though we know what he's going to say before he opens his mouth. I saw that Mum had stopped smiling, and I decided that she was remembering it, too.

Just as we were turning to leave, I saw Naomi. It didn't look like she'd been going around the shops or the market. She wasn't carrying any bags or anything. She was alone, coming towards the market from the older part of town where there weren't any shops. I wondered what she'd been doing and if I should go and say hi, but once again I decided not to. From the way that she kept her head turned away from me, I got the impression that she'd seen me and was hoping that I hadn't spotted her. But maybe that was me, being paranoid.

At school the next day she asked me what the market had been like.

'Pretty good,' I said. 'All the usual stuff. The toffee apples were great and I *might* have found a cool pressie for you.'

'Not another bobble hat?' she asked.

I shook my head and waited to see if she was going to say anything about what she'd been doing last night, but she didn't, so I changed the subject. Naomi was my best friend but that didn't mean that she needed to tell me everything. She could have secrets from me, and I certainly had some from her. No one could know everything about another person, and I don't think anyone would want to, anyway. It's better to keep some stuff to yourself.

'We'll go Christmas shopping another time. Maybe next week?' she said.

'Cool. You owe me a pressie.'

'Are you sure you want to know all this stuff?'

I was sitting opposite Kim, on one of his cool sofas.

I'd just asked him what was going to happen to Dad next. All the physical stuff – operations and things like that. I could guess most of it and it sounded horrific. I wasn't sure that I wanted to know, but wasn't it better to know for real, rather than go to bed every night imagining nightmare stuff? Some nights I woke up from dreams that my dad had been turned into a sort of

Frankenstein's monster with bits cut off and other bits stuck on.

'Would it make me a chicken if I don't find out?'

Kim uncrossed his legs.

'Not at all. All it means is that it's not the right time just now. One day it will be right. There's no medals for landing yourself with information you're not ready to handle. If that's how you're feeling right now, it's sensible to wait.'

I pretended I was thinking over what he'd said, but really I was relieved.

'How will I know when I'm ready?'

Kim smiled at me.

'You'll just know. It might be two months or two years. And when you're ready – even if we're not meeting any more – you can come back and talk to me about it, if you want to.'

'Thanks, Kim.'

I thought about what the bullies had said about Laura. About her being gay. Was she gay? Did it mean that Dad was, too?

'Is Dad gay?' I blurted the words out before I could think too much about them and chicken out of asking. This was something I needed to know.

'Gay? What would it mean for Dawn to be gay? That she likes men? Maybe to Dawn, being gay would mean liking women. Does it matter? Isn't finding love and happiness more important than the gender of the person who's making you happy?'

I shrugged.

'I guess so . . .'

'You know I'm gay, right? My partner's name is James. He's an architect. Does it make a difference? Do you not like me now? Think less of me? Think I'm a weirdo?'

More information to get my brain around. But of course I still liked Kim. It didn't make any difference.

'You're right,' I said. 'You're still Kim.'

Then we talked about what had happened since I'd last seen him – about me going to see Dad and freaking out, about meeting Laura and rescuing her from the bullies in the park and all the other stuff.

'That was a brave thing to do,' he said. 'And a foolish one, too. Did you think it was Dawn being attacked?'

'For a minute I did, but then I realised who it was. Laura's OK. She didn't deserve that kind of treatment.'

He thought for a bit.

'You don't seem to have much trouble accepting Laura for what she is. I hope that one day, you can do the same with Dawn. Maybe even get used to calling her that. It would mean a lot to her.'

'Maybe one day,' I said. 'Not yet. Maybe never. I don't know.'

That reminded me of something.

'My gran – Dad's mum, she died when I was ten – she *knew*! Dad said so when he was having a row with Grandad.'

'Are you surprised by that?'

'Well, yes,' I said. 'I thought old people would be disgusted and not understand at all!'

'Not necessarily. I don't think age has anything to do with it. It's more to do with attitudes to life. And how you feel about the person. And maybe how you feel about yourself, as well.'

'What's that got to do with anything?'

Kim looked at me for a long while.

'Let's just say that the more accepting someone is of themselves, the more likely they are to accept difference in others. Does that make sense?'

I didn't answer, thinking about Gran and her gardening wellies always covered in mud, and her messy hair and her crocheted toilet roll holder. If someone laughed at it (well, it was usually me, to be honest) she just smiled. Nothing seemed to upset her much. She didn't say much but if you spoke to her, you could tell she was listening. Naomi said once that there was a difference between hearing and listening and Gran *listened*. I think Grandad *hears*. He worries about what people think about him and hates being laughed at.

'I think I get it,' I said.

At the end of the session, as he walked me to the gate where Mum was waiting, I puzzled over the weird metal statue thingy for about the fiftieth time.

'Will you ever tell me what it's meant to be?'

He shook his head.

'It's like I said before. It's whatever you want it to be . . .'

I tilted my head to one side.

'Have you thought about putting some lights on it? It

could be a weird kind of Christmas tree. Quite suitable for this weird Christmas.'

Kim laughed.

'I'll bear that in mind,' he said.

'See you after Christmas?' I asked him.

He smiled. 'Sure. I'll be here.'

Chapter 23

A few days after that, I went into town after school with Naomi.

I thought we were going to get my Christmas present, and I was wondering if she had something in mind and hoping that it wasn't another soap on a rope, like the one she'd given me last year. I'd dropped it on my foot in the shower and it was black for a month. My foot, not the shower. It was lethal and it weighed a ton. The soap, not my foot.

When we walked past the chemist, I decided I was safe from deadly washing equipment. Then I thought maybe we were heading for WH Smith and I was wondering if she'd won the lottery and was going to get me a video game, in which case I'd have to buy something else to go with the friendship bracelet, but we went straight past that, too.

We headed through the square and out the other side. Maybe she wanted to go into the Burger Hut? But before we got that far she turned right down a little alley and on to a cafe called Buns and Baps. Normally we wouldn't be seen dead in there. It had lacy tablecloths and pictures of cats in clothes all over the walls. The windows were always steamed up, maybe because of the number of old ladies who liked to sit there, talking and talking and talking. I think it was their hot air that made the windows foggy.

Naomi stopped outside. I did too. I thought she looked a bit nervous and wondered if she'd volunteered to chat to lonely old ladies and was dragging me along to help out. She did things like that, sometimes.

Before I could think of a good excuse for ducking out of it, she blurted: 'There's someone who's waiting to talk to you. I want you to listen to what they've got to say.'

What was going on? Who was in there? I tried peering through the fogged-up windows to see if I recognised anyone, but all I could see were coats and blurred faces.

'You're not setting me up, are you? For reading to grannies or something?' I peered into Naomi's eyes. She met my gaze and held it.

'Trust me, Dan. You need to hear this.'

Without waiting for a reply she pushed the door open, setting a bell jangling. I followed, brain fizzing with all kinds of ideas about what was going on.

It was pretty dark in there, although there were quite a few fake Victorian lamps on the walls. They must all have been set to 'dim'. It was stuffy and there were too many people talking at the same time. I looked around but the only face I knew was Mrs Pollard, chatting to a couple of old biddies and scoffing scones with sultanas in. Typical. I detested sultanas. I could never forget that they were dead grapes. I was pretty sure Naomi hadn't brought me here for a meeting with *her*, so I kept on searching for someone else I knew.

'She'll be at the back where it's quiet,' Naomi said, and started edging her way among the tables.

She? Who was *she?* The only person I could think of was Hannah Sullivan. Maybe she'd asked Naomi to set us up? I hoped not, for lots of reasons. If it wasn't Naomi, I'd have been heading for the exit by then. I hated places like this, even without the secret meeting thing. But it *was* Naomi, and I trusted her, so I followed. Mrs Pollard looked up and saw me, but I turned my head and made it clear that I wasn't in the market for gossip over tea and dead grapes.

Once we were through the too-close tables and past a dresser stacked with blue and white china that I bet no one ever used, we turned right. It was cooler and quieter there. Only three tables, all widely spaced and only one of them was occupied.

By Laura.

My eyebrows snapped together. What was going on? I had nothing against Laura, I actually thought she was pretty brave, but that didn't mean I wanted to hang out with her.

'Naomi?'

She ignored me.

'Hi,' she said, when she reached Laura. She pulled out a chair. 'Sit down, Dan. Laura's got something to tell you.'

I wasn't angry, only confused, so I sat, expecting Naomi to plonk herself down next to me.

'This is for you to hear. I'll wait around the corner.' One reassuring smile and she walked away.

Laura looked OK today. Her jumper wasn't too frilly round the neck like the other one I'd seen her in. And she'd done better with her make-up. It was sort of quieter, more like Mum's. And Dad's.

'You look nice,' I said.

She looked pleased.

'Wow, that's a big compliment. Thanks.'

Right, I thought, I've done my bit and broken the ice. Now you've got to say something. I waited, but she looked awkward, turning over the froth on her coffee with her teaspoon.

'Are you OK after that thing in the park last week?' I asked, when it looked like she was never going to start saying whatever it was that she wanted to say.

'Yeah. Thanks again, Dan. You're a lifesaver. Literally, maybe.' She took a deep breath and carried on. 'Actually, that's related to what I want to say to you . . . what you did was really brave and I was a bit surprised that you risked so much for a stranger. But maybe you thought I was someone else? Someone you knew better?'

My heart did a flip in my chest.

'Someone else, like who?'

She opened her mouth and shut it again, two or

three times. If I hadn't been so freaked out, I'd have told her she looked like a goldfish.

She took a gulp of her coffee.

'I want to tell you about a friend of mine. There's a society in London for people like me. The people who work there, they put us in touch with others who are going through similar changes. Well, this society connected me with someone who lives fairly nearby. Names aren't important at the moment—'

'Woah!' I held up my hands. This was too close to home. I wasn't going to hang around to find out if this person she'd been talking to was Dad.

'I don't want to hear this.'

I stood up to go, but Laura put out one hand and held my arm.

'Want to and need to are two different things. I'm not saying this for me, Dan. I'm saying it for you. Because it might help you. Please . . .' we locked eyes, 'just sit down for two minutes?'

I thought for a long moment. Maybe it wasn't Dad. He'd said there were a few people like him around. If it wasn't him, it didn't matter what she said. If it *was* him, well, I could always say she'd got the wrong person. Part of me was thinking *what does she know? What's this thing that she needs to tell me?* There was only one way to find out.

I sat down.

Laura smiled. 'Good. OK . . . this person was in a state. Complete turmoil. Desperately unhappy and fed up with fighting the need to be someone else. They told me that this need had been with them for as long as they could remember and no matter what they did, or tried to do, they couldn't leave it behind. It was ripping them apart.'

She stopped and looked into my eyes, waiting to see if I was going to say anything. I didn't. I folded my arms and stared back at her.

'OK,' she sighed, like I was being awkward. 'This person had a family and they meant the world to them. Him. I'm sure you've guessed I'm talking about a man . . .' she stopped again and raised her eyebrows, waiting for me to say something.

I didn't. Couldn't. There was a frog-sized lump in my throat that would have stopped me talking even if I wanted to.

'When this man came to see me, just for a coffee and a chat, he was close to despair. "Not being me is killing me, but I can't hurt my family. They're more important than anything else. My wife, my . . . *son* . . . I don't know if I could live without them and they would be so hurt."'

I looked down, staring at the lace tablecloth like it was a treasure map I was trying to memorise, and biting the inside of my cheek.

'Then he started going on about looking for a cure. A lot of us – people like me and this other person – go through that stage when we realise that the change is inevitable. We just can't carry on as we are. It's horrible, because it means that you're seeing yourself as diseased. There is no cure, of course, because it's not an illness and we all come to terms with that in the end, or else we go under . . .'

I jerked up my head to stare at Laura. What did she mean? What was *going under*? Was she saying that Dad might have – I couldn't even let the words into my brain! My horror must have showed on my face, because she patted my hand.

'The reason I'm telling you this, Dan, is because I want you to know how much your dad loves you and your mum, and that if there was anything he could've done to stop what he's doing now, he'd have done it. Naomi came to see me to tell me that you're struggling. She thought I could help. I had no idea, when you bashed into me, that you were Dawn's son. Maybe it was fate that we met. I hope, when you've had a chance to think about what I've said, that it might make things a bit easier for you?'

All I was thinking at that moment was that I couldn't sit there any more. I needed to get away and think. I was up and stumbling towards the exit. I went past Naomi without a word, almost without seeing her. Some part of me realised that she'd got up and was hurrying after me.

I shoved through the maze of tables, knocking Mrs Pollard's arm just as she raised her tea to her lips. It must have sloshed over her sultana scones but I didn't stop to apologise.

Then I was outside. I was about to run off, but something stopped me. I stared down at the pavement, trying to work things out. I'd had enough of running away.

So I turned and watched Naomi slip through the door to join me. I took some deep breaths and felt my heart slow down.

'You OK?' she asked, frowning with worry.

I shrugged.

'I don't know yet, but I think you were right. I needed to hear that.'

I looked through the foggy windows at Laura, who was standing inside, watching us. I raised a hand.

'I'll think about it later,' I said. 'Let's go back in and have a hot chocolate with Laura. She looks like she needs calming down a bit.'

'No, I'm not angry with you,' I said to Naomi on our way home. 'You did it to help, and maybe it will. And anyway, I'm fed up with feeling angry all the time.'

Naomi gave a big sigh and threaded her arm through mine.

'Phew, that's a relief. When I went to see Laura last week – on Christmas shopping night – I was going to ask her to pretend she knew your dad. I thought you might listen to things from her that you wouldn't accept from anyone else. But she actually did know him! It's all true!'

'Poor Dad,' I said. 'I hadn't really thought about how hard things must have been for him. When I went to see him in his flat, he said it was like being a spy in disguise, waiting all the time to get found out. I wasn't interested at the time, but when you think about it, it must be really stressful – like being Ethan Hunt in *Mission: Impossible*! *He's* really jumpy!'

Naomi laughed at that, although I'm not sure why.

'There's always a movie for you, isn't there? To help you work the world out. And if there's no movie, there's something from nature – an animal or rare bug or something.'

I thought about that.

'Yeah, I suppose so. But why not? We're animals, too. Doing our thing, living our lives, trying to adapt.' I nudged her shoulder. 'There's nothing wrong with it, is there? You're not having a pop at me?'

'No, I'm not. Not at all. Actually, I think I'm a bit envious . . .'

We walked the rest of the way home in silence. My brain was whirring as I tried to take in what had just happened. And I think Naomi's was doing the same thing.

Chapter 24

The following weekend, Dad asked me to go Christmas shopping with him. Well, Mum asked me for him. I think he was scared I'd say no and had decided that getting Mum to do the asking would make it easier for me to refuse.

My first thought was no, I don't want to risk being seen with him, but then I remembered what Laura had said and I decided to do it. I'd never been out in public with Dad and it was about time I gave it a go.

So the next Saturday morning, Dad came and picked me up.

Mrs Pollard's curtains were twitching as we walked down the path, so I waved at her. They went still after that. I think I'd embarrassed her. She could stuff herself with sultana scones for all I cared. I didn't need her good opinion and neither did Dad.

Dad was dressed in a skirt and a long jumper and an even longer coat. I thought he looked OK, considering.

Better than Laura, anyway, who seemed to dress a bit like a granny.

'Do you want to go shopping here? Or in Abingdon?' he asked.

'Abingdon,' I said, straight away. There was less chance of being spotted by someone I knew there.

'I thought you might say that.' He must have worked out what I was thinking. I felt myself blushing.

'Do you have a list of what you need to get?' I asked, to cover my embarrassment. 'Do you know what you'd like for Christmas?' I crossed my fingers and hoped he wouldn't say a bra or perfume or something that would be weird to buy for him.

'There's a book I'd like. A new thriller. I'll show it to you.' That sounded good to me. Men and women both liked to read thrillers. I knew that Mum liked them, too.

'As for the list of what I've got to get, it's pretty short,' he continued. 'Just something for your mum and something for you.'

That made me remember that conversation I'd had with Naomi about kids with divorced parents who got two lots of Christmas and birthday presents. It seemed like a long time ago, but it was only a few weeks. When we'd had the conversation, I thought that getting double presents sounded cool but now it was happening to me, I realised that if it was a choice between extra presents and Dad, it was no contest. Although having Dad *and* extra presents would be best of all.

We drove to Abingdon in silence. I was thinking about what would happen when we got there, and maybe Dad was doing the same thing. In the quiet, I was imagining all kinds of horrible situations with Dad being recognised and attacked, or laughed at, or thrown out of the shops for being a freak, and me as well, because I was with him. But I was here now and there was no getting out of it. We would just have to see how it went.

We parked in the multi-storey and decided to go to the bookshop first. We got in the car park lift and a few seconds later, just as the doors were closing, someone shouted: 'Hang on!' and a couple with a little girl in a pushchair ran towards us. Dad punched the hold button. I could feel my palms starting to sweat as they scrambled into the lift. The man looked at Dad and muttered thanks. I waited for him to do a double take and start yelling at Dad or something, but he didn't. Maybe Dad really looked like a woman to anyone who didn't know him well. Or maybe the man *had* realised what Dad was and just didn't care. Maybe most people – apart from drunk, spotty bullies – didn't think it was a big deal.

The bookshop was crowded with Christmas shoppers and there was a queue of about a zillion people waiting for the till, but once again everyone seemed too busy with their shopping lists to notice us. We found the thriller Dad wanted on the *JUST IN!* shelves by the front door and then we went to the travel section and found a book about India that Dad was sure Mum would like. After that, we went to Natural History and I started looking at the big books of photos of elephants and whales and weird birds that looked like they'd been designed by cartoonists. I was so busy looking at them that I forgot about Dad, until he nudged me in the back.

'Anything you'd like?' he asked.

'I suppose so. They all look cool.'

So he made me turn my back while he picked one and then we went to join the queue for the tills.

There was a bit of a problem there but that was down to me, not Dad. He paid for his books and the lady behind the counter hadn't noticed anything wrong with him, or if she had she was a good actress. Then it was my turn to pay for Dad's book. And I didn't have enough money. I suppose I'd spent more than usual, with chips and Coke for Naomi and manga comics and things, and I realised that I hadn't had any pocket money that month.

I flushed the colour of Dad's nails.

'Oh,' I said, digging my hands into my jeans pockets to try and find some more cash. 'I haven't got enough . . . Could you?' I looked up at Dad.

He rolled and his eyes and handed over a ten-pound note.

'Kids!' the woman behind the counter said to him. 'They don't miss a trick, do they?'

And they both laughed.

That was when I started to think that maybe people didn't really look at other people. Or that when they did, they'd already decided what they were going to see and unless something went really wrong, they weren't going to see anything else.

As we walked around Abingdon, buying some bath bombs for Mum from me and a jumper from Dad that he said she would love, and some hi-top trainers for me, I decided that I was right. Most people didn't look at other peoples' faces at all, unless they had to because they bumped into each other or something.

I was starting to feel a lot more confident and relaxed about the whole being out with a transsexual thing, when I did collide with someone. Someone I knew. Maybe the last person on the entire planet that I'd want to bump into.

Josh Jacobs.

Chapter 25

It happened when we were coming out of the games shop.

I was feeling pretty good. Dad had just bought me the latest Monster Raider game and *still* we hadn't had any problems. I'd even started looking at people as we walked towards them, rather than doing the hiding-my-eyes-like-Nelson thing.

Dad had gone through the door first and was going on about getting a bottle of whiskey for Grandad and wondering if he'd just throw it back at him and whether he should save his money. I'd just had a text from Mum, asking how we were getting on and I was replying that everything was OK, so I wasn't looking where I was going. And *SMACK!* I bashed into the person coming into the shop as I was going out.

I looked up from my phone. I had my mouth open to say sorry but I shut it again when I saw that it was Josh. He'd been texting too.

'Look where you're going, loser,' he said, and he glared

at me. Then I think he must have been worried that I might be with an adult who would have heard him. He worries a lot about his image and likes everyone to think he's perfect. He started looking around.

Meanwhile, Dad had come to a halt and was watching us. I don't think he heard what Josh said, but he'd certainly noticed his son and this other boy glaring at each other. He took a step towards us but then he stopped. He was looking into my eyes and I think he was trying to work out whether I wanted him to say something or not. I shook my head.

But Josh followed my eyes. He saw Dad. His mouth fell open.

'Everything OK?' Dad asked.

Josh gave me a horrible smile.

'So, who's this, Dan?' he asked.

What should I say? My brain was fizzing with images of what Josh would do when he got to school on Monday, if he worked it out. He'd tell everyone that Dad was a transsexual. He'd jeer and laugh and that would make other kids do the same thing. I'd spend the rest of my school life as a freak. The son of a freak.

So I said, 'It's a friend.'

'A *friend*?' He gave that horrible smile again. It was *knowing*. I was imagining all kinds of things going through his mind. 'Interesting *friends* you've got, Dan.'

'I know. Aren't I lucky?' I said, to shut him up. 'Maybe you should get some interesting friends too. It would make a change.' Then I walked off without giving him a chance to reply.

Dad followed me.

I didn't look back, but I could feel Josh's eyes on my back. I wondered if he was already on his phone, spreading the news about Dan Yates and his lady-man friend.

At school on Monday, Josh was ready for me.

The Hedgehog was late into class, so there was no one there to stop him.

Josh started as soon as I walked through the door into Registration.

'Here he is, Cherrington's latest freak. How's your new *friend*, Dan?'

I felt my cheeks flaming. I couldn't help it. I wanted to kill Josh. He turned to Kyra and Ashley and Hannah. They were sitting on their desks and chatting while they waited for Sarcasmo to turn up.

'Have you heard? Dan's made friends with a lady man. They were out shopping together on Saturday, looking all cosy. In fact, he's friends with two lady men. There was that one he tried to help in the park the other day, too. What do you think? Do you reckon he's one as well? Do you reckon Dan's *gay?*'

Kyra and the others looked at me with astonished eyes. They didn't say anything.

I felt lots of things at once. One of them was shame, but there wasn't as much of that as I'd spent Sunday imagining. What I felt much more strongly was anger, and relief, too. The thing that had been scaring me for weeks was about to happen. At least I wouldn't be driving myself mad expecting it, any more. Once it had happened, I could start dealing with it. That had to be better.

Naomi walked in just as Josh was speaking.

I could feel my heart pounding in my chest. Maybe she heard it. She dumped her bag on her chair and came to stand next to me.

'Are you going to be a lady man as well, Dan?' Josh jeered again. 'Kyra, you can lend him your Cinderella costume. He'd look pretty in that. Be careful though. He'll be after your part in the panto next, and I don't fancy having to dance with *him*.' He gave a nasty laugh. I noticed that the others didn't join in. Maybe they were too surprised.

'Shut it, Josh,' Naomi said. 'Dan's friends are his business, no one else's.'

'Good job you've got Naomi to hide behind,' Josh went on. 'Tell you what, Naomi can wear her Prince Charming outfit and Dan can wear Kyra's Cinderella dress and you two can swap places. Not for the panto. I mean, every day. I'll be sure to look out for you in the park, wobbling around in high heels with your freaky lady men friends.'

Then three things happened at the same time. The door closed with a huge bang and Mr Hodges was standing there, purple in the face and looking like he was about to blow a fuse.

Meanwhile, Naomi was reaching for Josh. I think she was going to grab him round the throat. Hit him, maybe.

I grabbed Naomi and pulled her back. Not that Josh didn't deserve it, but I didn't want her getting into trouble because of a pathetic squirt like him.

'Joshua Jacobs!' Mr Hodges roared like a lion. 'I am *absolutely* appalled at—'

He didn't get any further because I didn't let him. I held up one hand. I'd spent weeks worrying and lying and feeling sick every time I thought that someone might find out. I was fed up with it. I thought about the courage Dad and Laura showed every time they went out. They never knew if someone was going to have a go at them or even attack them, like those bullies in the park. It was time for me to show a bit of courage too. Time for me to show I was my father's son. Time to take control.

'It's all right, sir,' I said, feeling terrified and relieved at the words about to come out of my mouth. 'Josh, you're wrong. It wasn't a friend. It was my dad. He's changing. Evolving. How about you do some evolving, too? Grow up a bit and get over it.'

I think I was talking to myself as much as Josh.

No one jeered. No one laughed. At first, no one seemed to know what to do.

Naomi was the first to move.

'That was brave,' she said, and pulled me into a hug.

Then, one by one, Hannah and Kyra and Ashley and nearly everyone in the class came up to me. Some of them touched me. Not hugged me, like Naomi, but put a hand on my arm or my shoulder. No one knew what to say.

I looked from Ashley's face to Hannah's and then all around. No one was looking disgusted. No one was looking anything except friendly and concerned.

No one apart from Josh. His face was kind of stiff and horrified at the same time, like Nelson's when we take him to the vet.

'Joshua Jacobs.'

He swivelled to look at Mr Hodges, who was scribbling something on a piece of paper.

'You'd better get along and explain your bigoted ideas to Mrs Llewellyn,' he said. 'Take this note with you. I'll be checking that you've delivered it.'

Josh's eyes filled with tears. He trailed over to the Hedgehog and took the note.

As he left the classroom, looking like a mouse on its way into a snake enclosure, I wondered if I should feel sorry for him.

I decided not to bother.

Chapter 26

The whole of school seemed to go mad on panto day. Lessons were interrupted as performers and helpers (me included) were pulled out to rehearse, and the hall was off limits while it was cleaned and polished up for parents. The Hedgehog was rushing around like an overwound clockwork toy. He was wearing an extra-special tie. It had Rudolph the Red-nosed Reindeer on it and when he pressed a button at the back, Rudolph's nose lit up and it played a tune. It was pretty sad, but he'd been growing on me since he'd stuck up for me with Josh, so I told him I liked it.

Since the Hedgehog had sent him to see Mrs Llewellyn, Josh had been pretty quiet. When he saw me now, he just looked the other way. The other kids had been fine with me, so far. Sometimes I saw someone looking at me and whispering into another kid's ear, and I was pretty sure I knew what they were talking about, but I decided I could live with that. It was pretty interesting, after all. Let them talk about it. Soon something else weird or interesting would happen and Dan Yates and his transsexual dad would be old news.

Today was Josh's big day and at breaktime you could hear him singing his panto song in front of a little crowd of girls. When he finished, they all clapped like he'd won *The X-Factor* or something. I just rolled my eyes at Naomi and hunched my shoulders as we walked past.

'I hope it goes as well tonight,' he was saying. 'It's actually the most important song in the whole panto!' I noticed that when he said 'actually' his voice squeaked a bit. He stopped and gave a cough to clear his throat. I hoped it was nerves. Maybe he'd get stage fright for the first time in his life and wouldn't be able to go on. That would teach him to pick on me. And to be nasty about transsexuals.

'I don't know how I put up with him,' Naomi muttered. 'You'd think he was a pop star waiting to hear if his song has gone to number one, rather than a kid with a part in a school panto.'

Apart from Josh, it was a fun day. Naomi and me both got to go into first lunch because there were more rehearsals that afternoon. We sat well away from Josh, but now and then I looked up and watched him. He seemed to be coughing a lot and rubbing his throat. Maybe he was getting a cold.

It was Christmas lunch day too, which put everyone in a good mood, even the teachers. Everyone had a cheap Christmas cracker with their lunch and there were loads of bangs as everyone pulled them, and then groans and laughs as people read out the crappy jokes they found inside. Naomi and me pulled ours together and we put on our paper hats. Naomi's was yellow and mine was pink, but I didn't mind. I was just laughing out of politeness at her lame joke when I looked up and saw the Hedgehog watching me. He gave me a really wide smile. I didn't know whether to be pleased or freaked out.

Rehearsals that afternoon went OK and at last it was time for the panto. Although I was behind the curtains, I still felt a bit nervous in case I dropped something or put the scenery in the wrong place.

I peered out from behind the curtains. The hall was packed. I couldn't see a spare seat. The orchestra were tuning up. At least, I think they were. Maybe they were playing some pre-panto music but not very well. Mrs Llewellyn was at the piano, as usual.

I scanned the crowd and saw that Mum and Naomi's mum were sitting together. And they weren't alone. Dad – I still couldn't call him Dawn – was sitting in between them, chatting with them. I'd asked Mum to invite him.

He looked a bit nervous, but he was being brave and sticking it out. A few of the other parents looked at him, but most of them just did what they always did. Talked among themselves and tried to convince whoever they were sitting next to that their son or daughter was the most important kid in the show, even if they were just in the chorus. Or working behind the scenes.

At last, the tuning up ended. Mrs Llewellyn got up and said welcome to everyone and talked about how much work had gone into the pantomime. She thanked the Hedgehog for writing and directing it, and he stood up and waved and flashed his Rudolph tie.

And then we were off.

It started in a wood, with the seven dwarfs moaning because they'd lost Snow White and now there was no one looking after them. They got the audience laughing as soon as they came on because there were only four of them and they were all tall Year 11s. They sang a song called 'Try a *Little* Tenderness' and that made people giggle because every time they sang 'little' they shouted it really loud.

Then it was Kyra McGee as Cinderella and she did a dance and sang a song about waiting for her prince to come, but she sang *prints* instead of *prince* and said she'd taken a load of photos to be developed and they'd got lost in the post. That was quite good. The dance was wet, though. She was trying to look sad or romantic or something, but I thought she looked more like she had eaten something that had gone off and was going to throw up.

After that the curtains closed and we had about five seconds to change the scenery. We made quite a bit of noise as we dragged the painted trees off stage and replaced them with the grey stone walls of a castle. That made the audience laugh, too, although Mr Bennett looked a bit fed up.

This was Naomi's big bit, and she was brilliant. She looked cool in her silk coat and pink breeches. It was strange because the men's clothes made her look prettier, although I suppose she was quite pretty to begin with.

She did a dance with Cinderella and then she sang her song.

I'd heard her sing in rehearsals. The song was about being a hero and always being ready for action. She sang it well. But now she'd added another verse. This one went like this:

> *Not all heroes look like he-men*
> *Bulging biceps, cheesy grin*
> *Other heroes can be wee men*
> *Short and weedy, pale and thin.*
> *Women too are often heroes*
> *Being brave from morn till night*
> *Even kids can be heroic*
> *Never giving up the fight.*
> *Then there's folk who go through changes*
> *Some without and some within*
> *Facing fear and hate from strangers*
> *When their tolerance grows thin.*
> *Clothing, hair or creed or gender*
> *Heroes change because they must*
> *Vowing never to surrender*
> *To blind hatred and mistrust.*

The audience loved it. They lapped it up like Nelson with a bowl of ice cream. Mum and Dad clapped loudest of all. When Naomi finished and she was taking her bow, she looked into the wings and smiled at the Hedgehog. He gave her a grin and a thumbs up. Then he turned to me and did the same thing. Naomi caught my eyes and gave me a tiny wink. She had put that verse in for me and the Hedgehog was in on it, too. I wanted to hug her for a long time. Later on I would, I decided.

After that it was Josh's turn. He was Puss in Boots and he strode around stage like he owned it. I have to admit, his boots were cool, but someone had made some cardboard cat ears and stuck them on his head and he looked more like a bat than anything else. He had whiskers painted on his face too, and the end of his nose looked like he'd dipped it in some black paint.

He had some lines with Cinderella and I thought his voice sounded weird. A bit like someone was strangling him. From my place in the wings I could see his eyes opening wider and wider, like he was surprised or scared. Then the dwarfs came back on and made people laugh by chasing him around the stage, trying to get him to be their pet. Finally they got fed up and stomped off, leaving him to sing his song.

By now, I thought he looked terrified, which was unusual. He loved being the centre of attention. He started off OK:

It's not easy being a cat
And a hero one at that . . .

But then something went wrong. He started singing the next line:

It's not all chasing mice and having f—

and suddenly his voice cracked and he stopped singing. The orchestra stopped too and there was a silence, and then he tried again.

It's not all chasing m—

Same thing. He sounded like Nelson when he meets another cat and they're about to have a fight. Someone in the audience gave a little laugh, like they thought he was doing it on purpose, but most of them just sat there and murmured to each other.

Josh looked like the world had just ended.

'My voice . . .' he said, sounding much more grown up than he usually did. It seemed to startle him.

'My voice – it's broken. I can't go on!' He made it sound like he was announcing a massive tragedy.

The Hedgehog hurried out of the wings and took one of his arms and led him backstage, while the audience gave him a quick round of applause and then the panto continued. I don't think people thought any more about Josh. It was a big deal to him, but to other people it was just life.

As the Hedgehog comforted Josh, who was snivelling and making the black paint on his nose run in snotty streaks, I thought that this was one panto I'd never forget.

And neither would Josh.

Chapter 27

It was Christmas Eve, and Mum and me had finally got round to decorating the Christmas tree.

Usually it was Dad who went up into the loft to get it while we stood beneath the trapdoor, waiting for him to lower the tree and the boxes of decorations down, shivering in the cold air that crept down with them. It always seemed to be Arctic up there.

This year I stopped Mum as she put one foot on the loft ladder.

'I'll do it,' I said.

I don't think I'd ever been up there before. It was dark and cobwebby and full of junk, just like in scary movies before the monster jumps out. I wasn't frightened, though. It didn't take long to spot what I was looking for and I lowered the boxes down to Mum and then made my way back down the ladder.

Mum was looking a bit watery-eyed and I knew that she was thinking about Dad.

'It's freezing up there,' I said, blowing on my fingers. 'Some things never change.'

'Others do though.' She wiped one hand across her eyes. 'Come on, let's put on *Muppet Treasure Island* and get this tree decorated.'

That's kind of a Christmas tradition in our house. We decorate the tree while *Muppet Treasure Island* is playing. I've loved that movie since I was a kid. I think it's all the weird singing animals.

Outside it was already getting dark and the street was really quiet, like it always seems to be at Christmas. Mum drew the curtains and found the movie while I got the tree out of the box. We blew the dust off it and put it together and fluffed up all the branches, which always takes ages, and then it was time to get out the decorations.

The first thing out of the box were the lights – plain and white and round. They looked a bit like snowballs when they were plugged in. While Mum was unravelling them, she looked up at me.

'This reminds me. I went to see Kim yesterday and guess what? He's covered that sculpture in his garden with fairy lights. It actually looked quite pretty for a change. Nice idea, I thought!'

That made me feel good. Kim was always suggesting things to me and now I'd suggested something to him and he'd actually done it.

With the lights in place, we started on what Mum called the background decorations. These were small glass balls in silver and gold and red and purple. Not very interesting. We always put these on first and then added the special things last, in the places where they stood out best.

The special decorations had a box of their own. As I went to pull the tape off it, Mum disappeared into the kitchen.

'I think I need a glass of wine,' she said.

I could understand that. Our special Christmas decorations were full of memories. Without Dad, unpacking them and finding their spots on the tree was going to feel weird. I heard her open the drawer to get out the corkscrew and the *pop!* as she opened the bottle.

When she came back, the glass was already a quarter empty.

'Mum, about the wine . . .'

She put the glass down.

'I know, Dan. I'm drinking too much. I'll slow down, I promise. I've already cut down a bit.'

I thought about that. There weren't so many empty bottles in the kitchen, waiting to be recycled. That was a good thing.

'Maybe you can help me?' she said.

'How?'

'Just tell me if you think I'm overdoing it? OK?'

'OK,' I said. That would be easy.

The first thing we found in the box of special decorations was a ginger kitten, made of felt and with a loop of checked ribbon on its back to hang it from the tree. Mum had bought it to mark Nelson's first Christmas with us.

'Dad's not the only one who's changed,' I said, as I placed it on the tree.

Mum laughed and took a sip of wine and poked the real Nelson with her toe. He was already checking out the tree, deciding which of the decorations he would attack first. He just can't resist them. I think his mission in life is to destroy as many of them as possible.

Then she pulled out a packet of long glass icicles. There used to be loads of these but every year there seemed to be fewer.

'Nelson's had most of these,' Mum said.

'And Dad broke two or three last year, playing Twister.' I thought for a moment. 'Do you think he'll want to play Twister tomorrow?'

Mum shrugged.

'Probably. You know it's his . . . I mean, her favourite Christmas game.'

Dad was having Christmas lunch with some friends. One of them was Laura. Dad was coming to see us afterwards. When I'd asked Mum to invite Dad, she hadn't been too sure.

'You know your grandad's coming. What if they have another argument?'

'Then we'll chuck them both out. Tell them to come back when they've grown up. I'll do it if you don't want to. Or we'll make them both play Twister. They'll be laughing too much to argue.'

The next decoration to be unpacked was green glass, but this one was special. It was shaped like a teardrop and there was a sort of glass cave set into one of its sides.

This cave was full of colours: purple and red and gold. It was very old.

'My dad's favourite,' Mum sighed. Both of Mum's parents were dead and I'd never known them.

'Put it somewhere where you'll see it every day,' I said, as she took another sip of wine.

It took time to find the right places for all the special decorations. By the time we'd worked it out, Miss Piggy and Kermit were hanging upside over a cliff, singing a wet song about love leading them to where they were. I used to like it, but not any more. I'd moved on.

That just left the nativity set, carved out of wood. I was never that interested in Mary and Joseph and baby Jesus, laying in what looked like a supermarket basket. I liked the animals though. There were loads of them: not just sheep and cows and donkeys but peacocks and wolves and zebras and polar bears and giraffes. There was even a cat with some tiny kittens. I reckon that whoever had carved the set had been making a Noah's ark at the same time and had put some of the ark animals into the nativity for a laugh. If the stable in Bethlehem had reallyncontained all those animals it would have to be the size of a superstore. And the bears and wolves would fight each other and hunt the other animals and everyone would be knee deep in dung in about a day. It would be carnage.

The nativity set always went on one of Mum's Indian tables, against the wall to make it harder for Nelson to attack it. But this year, I had an idea.

'How about putting it on top of the bookcase, for

a change? It's higher than the table which will make it harder for Nelson to destroy.'

Mum liked the idea and I set to work, unwrapping the figures and putting them in their places. It was good to see the snarling wolves and the bears standing on their hind legs again. I decided to have some fun, and arranged them so it looked like the bears were attacking the peacocks and I swapped the mother cat for a wolf, so it looked as if the kittens were being brought up by a she-wolf, just like Mowgli in *The Jungle Book*.

Then I put Jesus in the shopping basket near the centre, because Mum would tell me off if I didn't, with Mary bending over him with a soppy look on her face. I picked up Joseph and was just going to put him between the zebras when I noticed something.

'Mum,' I said. 'I've never really noticed before, but Joseph is wearing a dress.'

Mum put down her wine glass and came to look.

'I think all the men wore dresses back then. Trousers weren't invented until much later.'

That made me think.

'So if Dad could go back in time, he'd look the same as everyone else?'

She gave a short laugh.

'Yes, I suppose he would.'

'That would solve our problems, wouldn't it?' I said.

'Only some of them. There'd still be the problem with him wanting to be a woman.'

'He's not gonna change his mind, is he? And we can't cure him . . . Mum?'

She just raised her eyebrows.

'Do you think everything will be sorted out by next Christmas?'

She went back to her wine glass and took another small sip.

'One way or another. Yes, I'm sure it will be.'

'And you won't stop me seeing him if you two don't get back together? If I still want to? Because I think I will.'

'I'd never do that. He's your dad. He always will be. I'd rather you knew him and knew you were loved, than grew up thinking that he'd dumped you when he started his new life.'

I looked at her with her funky jumper and half-full glass of wine and sad expression. Suddenly I wanted to give her a hug, so I did.

'I think that goes for you, too,' I said. 'He loves you as well. I don't think that will change.'

She looked surprised for a second and then hugged me back, really tightly. A bear hug.

'Dad's not the only one changing. You're growing up.'

'Maybe I'm evolving,' I said. 'Like Dad. I expect you're evolving too, but you probably won't notice it. It's like Darwin said: we have to change to survive. I think the three of us will be OK, one way or another.'

'Yes,' Mum said, putting down her wine glass. 'I think you're right.'

She picked up the remote.

'Tell you what,' she said, 'why don't we watch

something different for a change? Something new? The new Wonder Woman's meant to be great. It's streaming now, I think.'

'Good idea. Let's start a new tradition.'

Acknowledgements

My thanks to everyone involved in the publication of *Evolution*. Special thanks to Carsten, my agent, for his tenacity and encouragement, and to Elaine at Zuntold, for her insightful editing and belief in this heartfelt story.

For other insightful books,

head to

Zuntold.com